Papa's Girl Emmeline

PAPA'S GIRL
EMMELINE

Margaret Nyhon

Willow Press

To my great grandmother Sarah Fell, my grandmother Christian Marris, and my mother Joice Fell Mackie.

My darling Emmeline,

You based your life around your heroine,

but sadly you were let down by your dreams.

Contents

Chapter 1.
Emmeline

1

Chapter 2.
Papa's Life

5

Chapter 3.
Emmeline's Heroine, Isabella

10

Chapter 4.
Papa's Last Days

13

Chapter 5.
Emmeline's Life Change!

25

Chapter 6.
Disaster at a Colliery

35

Chapter 7.
Mr Ewan Thomas Fletcher

50

Chapter 8.
Filling the Vacant Positions at the Colliery

58

Chapter 9.
A Visit to Belle Isle

64

Chapter 10.
Emmeline's Seventeenth Birthday

74

Chapter 11.
Feelings are Stirring within Emmeline
91

Chapter 12.
Mr Stenhouse
99

Chapter 13.
A Sudden Call-out
109

Chapter 14.
Is Something in the Air?
115

Chapter 15.
Will the Truth be Revealed?
134

Chapter 16.
Was Emmeline's Dream about to Happen?
149

Chapter 17.
The Unspeakable Truth
161

Chapter 18.
Emerald Isle — the Warming Party
175

Chapter 19.
Emmeline's Wedding
191

Chapter 20.
A New Era
205

Chapter 21.
The Finale
227

About the Author
231

Other Books by the Author
232
Acknowledgements
233

1

Emmeline

Emmeline's background was full of history. She was only just starting to learn about her ancestors now that she was aged sixteen, and as her papa was very ill, he wanted her to know how he had acquired a lot of his wealth, some of which had come down through the generations. Since she had already lost her mama at a young age, this was going to be another blow to this young girl's life. Each day her papa told her more of his background and the prominent people who were part of their lives. She had been put into boarding school when her mama died, as her papa was otherwise occupied with his collieries, as they consumed his life. Perhaps this was, in fact, to hide that he was still in mourning over losing his wife.

It was the end-of-year break for Emmeline as school had finished and now she was home caring for her sick papa in their stately home. There were only two servants left — the groundsman and the maid, who would cook meals when required to do so. The maid, Jane, was a family friend who had worked in this household for many years, as did her mother. Emmeline's mother had offered them work through the Quakers, a Christian group of which she was a member. If you were known to be a Quaker, work was hard to come by, as the local Church of England members were against this new religious organisation that was invading their town.

Emmeline's grandmama was deeply involved in the Quaker movement, as her relative Margaret Fell owned Swarthmoor Hall. This 16th-century manor on the outskirts of Ulverston was famous for its association with the founding of Quakerism, and with George Fox, the founder of this movement. Swarthmoor Hall, run by Margaret, welcomed frequent travellers. While her husband was away a lot on business, Margaret allowed George Fox, who at that time was just beginning on a career of preaching his version of a simpler form of Christian worship, to stay there. She became swayed by this man's new reasoning, but her husband did not share her enthusiasm. Margaret opened her boarding house as the new meeting place for the Quakers; it became their headquarters. When her husband died, Margaret married George Fox. She was ten years his senior and had eight children. It was hard for Quakers to get work so Emmeline's grandmama hired Quakers to work for them. When Margaret Fell died, her estate was forfeited because of her connection to the Quakers, and it took her son years to obtain a 'grant of estates'.

Emmeline loved her life at boarding school. She was the storyteller. On special nights she would be seen sitting cross-legged on her bed while the other girls sat on the dormitory floor, all gathering around her bed listening to her stories. She was their heroine. They were all at puberty stage and feelings were stirring in their bodies, so romance was first and foremost on their minds. But none of the girls had such romantic family members as Emmeline. Their favourite story was her favourite, so it was told a thousand-fold; no one tired of it. She lived her second cousin Isabella's life through and through many times and now it became her life. She knew what her future held ... or did she? Her life was very much like that of her heroine. Her papa was very wealthy like Isabella's, their mothers had passed away while they were very young and they were both sole beneficiaries to their papas' estates. This, of course, made them heiresses to vast fortunes, and very much in demand by potential suitors, not excluding family members. Large fortunes passed down through families and these grew if uncles and aunts didn't marry, as their estates went back to their siblings. This had happened several times in Emmeline's family. She had just learnt of her great-uncle Richard Fell's windfall that was bestowed on the family. Her papa had told her this story just yesterday. No wonder she was a storyteller, as she had so many to tell.

Yesterday's story was not of a romantic nature, but it did make her excited, and it was another story for her school friends. Her great-uncle, Richard Fell, lived at Windermere and he loved to make money. He lived in a prominent home with a large model of a fox's head on the wall. He had horses and wagonettes and took visitors up over Kirkstone Pass, which was the way from Windermere to Potterdale and Ullswater. One winter, Lake Windermere froze solid and he designed non-slip studs for horses, thus allowing him to take people across the lake to Tarn Hows. When he died, all his household effects were sold off apart from an old mattress, which was to be burnt. As it was being carried to be set fire to, it was noticed there was a patch on the mattress revealing a hideaway. In the hideaway was found 1500 gold sovereigns and 1500 old pound notes, money he had hidden, being the fares he charged while taking the people across the frozen lake. This was so he didn't have to pay taxes. This money along with his estate came back to his siblings, as he had no family. As the families were large and many siblings did not marry, fortunes remained in the families.

2

Papa's Life

Emmeline's papa had married a much younger woman, in fact she was only eighteen. He was now in his early sixties, and was a very sick man. His family, the Christians, originated from the Isle of Man. They were a very prominent family and were called the First Deemsters, effectively judiciary heads administering the unwritten laws of the island. The family obtained valuable land and gathered power in political, legal and religious positions. Emmeline and her father now lived in Bowness in Cumbria. This was her most favourite area of all, as she would walk down to Lake Windermere and sit and look out over her Belle Isle and close her eyes and dream of her heroine, as this was her island. The isle was covered in beautiful trees, among them copper beeches and huge oaks, partially hiding the circular mansion that belonged to Isabella Curwen.

Emmeline's favourite room in their stately home was

the drawing room, only because a portrait of Isabella adorned the end wall. She would pull up one of the purple velvet chairs and tuck her legs under her body and stare for hours at her heroine. These were special moments as they brought back treasured memories of her time spent with her mama. She was the one who passed the stories of Isabella on to her. Papa had told her it was not the original painting that was commissioned to be painted by George Romney, who was a family friend, but it was still worth a lot of money. Emmeline didn't mind; it was still her favourite. In the background was Isabella's stately circular mansion on Belle Isle. This was Emmeline's dream come true. Her isle was going to be called Emerald Isle, and from there her dreams went on and on ...

She loved the romance of the two cousins vying for Isabella's attention, but sadly the one who loved her most was the one that lost out. This was to Emmeline's way of thinking. At boarding school, they had taken votes on who Isabella should have chosen and the votes swayed unanimously towards Fletcher instead of John. Was it because John was the wealthy one and that Fletcher's family had been bailed out financially by John?

Today was a beautiful warm day so she propped her papa up in his bed, so he could lie and watch her walking down to the lake. As she walked she would stop, turn around and wave to him and she would see his frail hand waving back. She loved him, as he was all she had left. Today was another dream day. She perched on her favourite mound and watched the sun dancing on the water, making it change its moods many times. One moment it was perfect and within seconds it seemed angry, then it seemed to smile again. This was caused by the odd cloud passing and shutting out the sun, which annoyed the water, so it let it be known. She could almost hear the water whispering to her.

Emmeline would look out across the lake to all the little islands, seventeen in all. This did not include Belle Isle — it wasn't just an island, it was an enchanted island which belonged to Isabella, and it was the only one that had been inhabited. But one day another island would be inhabited and that was going to be Emmeline's Emerald Isle. Her favourite saying, written by a poet, one she would sing over and over again, was: 'Give me six hundred pound a year, and Curwen's Isle on Windermere'. When she sung this to herself she felt a closeness to the lake, which made her feel warm deep down inside. She closed her eyes and relaxed, leaving the outside world behind. She spent hours in her own little fairy-tale world, because this was her happy place.

Up until sixteen, she had lived a very sheltered life. Boarding school had kept her away from the outside evils and each holiday she would come home to her papa and her beloved Lake Windermere. She had cousins that came to visit her at times, and a couple of uncles who were always visiting Papa lately discussing business with him; as he was too ill to worry about very much now, she thought they looked after his finances. Emmeline had no idea of her family's wealth as it had not been discussed with her; she thought her uncles knew all about it!

As she made her way back to her home, she looked for her papa's wave but she could not see him, so thought he must have fallen asleep. In the driveway was a strange carriage, one she hadn't seen before. As she entered through the large entrance hall she heard voices, then she saw her papa in his wheelchair at his office desk with a strange man. There were papers everywhere. "Come here, darling Emmeline, I want you to meet Mr Edward Stenhouse. He is my solicitor. We are going through my estate; he will look after my affairs when I am not here." "But, Papa, you are going to get better, I will stay home and look after you," sobbed Emmeline. "No, Emmeline, I am a very sick man, but you will never have to worry about money. Mr Stenhouse will see to that. We have discussed what is to happen to my collieries and my estate," replied her papa. Emmeline looked at this stranger. His eyes were small as they were partly hidden by his bushy eyebrows. He scared her a little as he had a nervous twitch, which made him a bit jumpy. She guessed he would be middle-aged, but in actual fact he was only in his early thirties. All she knew about him was he was Papa's solicitor, that was all she needed to know.

When he left she tidied up her papa's desk and then wheeled him through to the drawing room. "Papa, did Mama actually know Isabella?" asked Emmeline. "No, my darling daughter, she died when your mother was very young, but she had visited Belle Isle. She rowed out in a little row boat to the enchanted isle and walked among the beautiful trees that John Christian Curwen had planted. He adored his beloved Isabella; this was his gift to her. As he had access to all her wealth as well as his, he probably bought the island with her money. She was Isabella Curwen of Workington Hall. They were a very wealthy family, as you know; she was my older cousin," he explained. "You know, Papa, one day I am going to be like Isabella and have my own island; it will be called Emerald Isle," Emmeline told her papa. This was her dream, but in actual fact she had the wealth to make this a reality, not that she knew this at the time. "One day, your dream may come true, my darling daughter," her papa told her.

The school holidays had finished and Emmeline was back at boarding school. She didn't want to leave her beloved papa as he was ill, but he insisted she finish her education. Here she was once again sitting cross-legged on her bed with all the girls sitting on the floor waiting for more wonderful stories to be told. She was happy she had a new story to tell them about her Great Uncle Richard. The girls all gasped as she revealed about the fortune hidden in the mattress and to think it could have been burnt and no one would have known. How exciting! They wanted to know if she had met any young men while she was at home. Sadly, she had to tell them the only man she had met was her father's solicitor and he was middle-aged and not at all charming, as he had a twitch that made him jumpy. Anyway, she didn't need to meet anyone; she had Isabella and Belle Isle, and that was all she needed to keep her happy at the moment. This is what brought her the most happiness at this time in her life.

3

Emmeline's Heroine, Isabella

Isabella was the daughter of Henry Curwen. Her mother had died when she was very young, and she lost her papa at age sixteen. She was placed under the guardianship of her two aunties Jane and Bridget Christian. She was the heiress to Workington Hall and she had inherited interests in large mining operations, leaving her a very wealthy young lady, which attracted many young and not-so-young suitors. She had two cousins that were attracted to her, but as she grew older she was drawn more to her 'prodigious' cousin, John Christian. The other cousin Fletcher Christian's family had suffered financially, so cousin John had bailed them out. She preferred the company of Fletcher when she was younger; they were sweethearts.

Isabella was sent away to school in London, as John was not thought to be suitable for her. He was ten years her senior and had been married to another wealthy heiress to whom he had a son. After she died, Isabella became his latest attraction. But the two could not be kept apart so they ran away to Scotland to marry. Later, they did sanctify their marriage in the parish church of St Mary Magdalene. John quadrupled the Curwen fortune and spent a lot of money turning Workington Hall into a mansion befitting his social position. He changed his surname from Christian to Curwen, by royal licence, and became known as John Christian Curwen. They bought the island in Lake Windermere and called it Belle Isle after Isabella. Meanwhile, her cousin Fletcher Christian was broken-hearted when he learned that John had married Isabella, so he took his bitterness to sea. Although his family were an old, established Cumbrian family, imprudent investments by his brothers eroded the family fortune. His mother's family, the Fletchers, owned Moorland Close, not far from Cumbria's Lake District, situated near the banks of the Derwent River and the town of Cockermouth. Fletcher signed on as a midshipman and sailed to India. A career in the navy offered the opportunity for him to rise to a position of influence, thus signing on with Captain Bligh as master's mate on the *Bounty*. The rest was history and from this arose the 'mutiny on the *Bounty*'. He had cast Captain Bligh adrift with some of his crewmen. Fletcher took a Tahitian wife called Mi'mitti, whom he renamed Isabella, renewing rumours that he had never gotten over his love for his cousin, Isabella.

The remaining nine mutineers, six Tahitian men and eleven Tahitian women left Tahiti and settled on Pitcairn Island. Fletcher went on to have three children, Thursday October, Charles and a daughter Jane Ann. Thursday and Charles were the ancestors of almost everybody with the surname Christian on Pitcairn and Norfolk islands. Fletcher died aged twenty-eight and was thought to have been seen in the Lakes District of Cumbria. There is no known burial place. As well as a love story, there was a lot of history that came with Emmeline's background.

John and Isabella went on to have eight children, all taking the surname of Curwen. Isabella died at the age of fifty-four. This was Emmeline's school friends' favourite story.

4

Papa's Last Days

Emmeline was a good student, as she wanted to please her papa. She was not into activities; she would rather spend her time daydreaming or reading romantic books. Her teachers often talked among themselves about the stories she wrote, and could see the potential of her becoming a writer. She was very popular among her peers. No one talked about wealth at boarding school; they were there as students and to study, they were as one. She only ever wanted to be a writer, to put her thoughts and stories into books so they would be remembered for many years. Her cousins thought she was boring, as she would just daydream the hours away with nothing concrete to show, but in her own mind she was achieving plenty. They wouldn't know where their lives were going to take them, but Emmeline knew exactly what path her life was going to take, because in her own mind she was living Isabella's life. The two lives had been similar up until thus far.

At mid-term break she said goodbye to her school friends as she climbed onto the horse-drawn carriage that had been sent to bring her home. Papa had arranged this, as his health was worsening. As the carriage pulled up at the stately home her two uncles were there to greet her and warn her that her papa was not at all well. The doctor was with him at that very moment. Emmeline ran into the home calling to her papa. "Papa, Papa, I'm home, are you all right?" When she entered his bedroom, she could see that he was very ill and the doctor was attending to him. "I'm home, Papa, I will look after you. Please get well," she pleaded. "My darling Emmeline, come and sit with me," he asked of her. The doctor was listening to his chest; his breathing was very shallow and his pulse was slowing down. It wouldn't be long before everything shut down. The doctor decided not to say anything to Emmeline as she would be so upset; it was better to leave her with hope in her heart in his final hours. He would just close his eyes and drift off to sleep. This was her special time with her beloved Papa. "Is Papa going to get better?" she asked the doctor. "We will just have to wait and see," he said, not wanting to dampen her hopes until it was all over. As he left the room, the two uncles were waiting for a verdict from him. He could see the eagerness of them to know what was happening to their brother, but he wanted Emmeline to be there with him for his final hour. "He has requested for Emmeline to sit with him, so I ask you to leave the two of them together for the time being," was the information he offered them.

He had seen vultures before many times; he knew what they looked like and here were two of them in this room. He knew Emmeline's Papa was extremely wealthy, as his wealth was well known among the townspeople. Poor

Emmeline, what was ahead for her? he wondered. "I will stay for a cup of tea," he said to the men, forcing them to stay with him. He knew by the time he had finished his cuppa that Emmeline's Papa would have drifted off into his final sleep and he would be here to do his final duties.

Meanwhile, Emmeline was talking to her papa not for one moment thinking the end was near. She was telling him about her Emerald Isle when he took her hand and whispered, "The collieries you must keep; find Thomas!" She felt him squeeze her hand. "I will let you sleep now, Papa, you are tired," and she bent down and gave him a kiss. She walked out into the drawing room and there was the doctor and the two uncles. "Papa is sleeping now," she said. With this the doctor stood up and went into the bedroom and did his final duties. Emmeline's papa had passed away. The doctor came back into the drawing room to announce that Mr Christian had passed away. "No, Papa, don't leave me, please don't leave me!" she sobbed as she ran to his bedside, but she knew it was too late. The doctor stood beside her. "I'm so sorry, Emmeline, but he is at peace now, there will be no more pain. Do you have somewhere to go?" With this the uncles offered her to go home with them. "Thank you but I want to stay here; this is my and Papa's home. He would want me to stay here," she answered. "But you are only sixteen, Emmeline, you cannot be here on your own," said the doctor. "I will ask Jane to come and stay with me," she said. "No, you must come home with us, and we can sort out your father's finances," suggested the uncles. The doctor was right in his thinking; the vultures couldn't wait to start their feasting. "Perhaps Emmeline would be better here if Jane will come and stay with her," he suggested. He watched the dismayed look on the uncles' faces.

Emmeline went and sat with her papa as she didn't want him to be on his own; she would wait until the funeral people came and took him away. She knew where he wanted to be buried as they had walked up the hill many times and sat and looked over the lake. She remembered his words: "When my time is over, bring me up here, so I can watch over our beloved Windermere." They both shared the same love for the Lakes District; this was their home. She wondered what she would do now. Then her mind went back to her papa's last words, 'find Thomas' — who was Thomas? She had never heard him mention this name before; where would she find him?

When Jane heard about Mr Christian passing away, she came straight away to be with Miss Emmeline, as she knew how much they loved each other. She hoped Miss Emmeline would cope; nothing ever got on top of her as she just dreamed her way through life. But this was way bigger than anything she had ever faced, as she was too young to remember much about her mama's passing. When the funeral people came to take her beloved papa away in the horse-drawn carriage, she stood at the entrance and cried. Jane stood with her arms around Emmeline. Emmeline's two uncles were in Papa's office sorting through papers. As she walked past the desk she said to them, "Papa's solicitor has all his important papers; he took them away with him." They looked at her and asked what his name was. She said she didn't know, as she wasn't ready to discuss any of her papa's business at the moment. She was too sad. She called out to Jane and told her she was going to sit by the lake for a bit, she would be back soon. As she walked down she never stopped and looked back, because her papa wouldn't be there to wave to her any more. Emmeline sat in her favourite place and looked across to Belle Isle with a heavy heart. What would she do now? Would she go back to school or stay and look after Papa's home? She would miss her school friends but things were different now; she had to think about life outside of boarding school. Papa had the collieries, and he had asked her to keep them; perhaps she could learn about these. Mr Stenhouse was there to help her; Papa had told her that. But first she had to bury her beloved Papa. She wondered who she could ask about Thomas; perhaps Jane would know, as she had been at their home for many years. She closed her eyes and her thoughts went straight to Isabella. How did she feel when she lost her papa? Would she have been sad just like me? she asked herself. With that she sat and sobbed her little heart out. How similar their lives were, although they were a generation apart.

She was suddenly brought out of her daydream when she felt something wet on her face. She sat upright only to find a dog licking her. "Come here, boy," yelled a voice from a distance. Emmeline looked up to see a young gentleman walking along the lake front, holding the hand of a young boy. "Oh, I'm sorry about that," he said as he came near. He could see her tear-stained face and asked if she was okay. Emmeline burst into tears, unable to control herself. He came up to her and sat down. "I'm sorry, is it something I said?" he asked. The little boy sat down next to him and asked why the lady was crying; was she hurt? "I have just lost my papa," she sobbed. The man said sympathetically, "I know how you feel. I lost my wife and my little son has lost his mother. You will feel sad for a long time but it will pass. Life has to go on; we all have dreams to fulfil." Emmeline wondered if she had heard right; did he mention dreams? "Are you a dreamer?" she asked. "Yes, I dream of many things; life is built on dreams. Imagine people who don't dream, how sad that must be," he replied. "See that island over there?" he said. "I dream about that every day." "Do you mean Belle Isle?" she asked. "Is that what it is called? What a lovely name. Who is it named after?" he asked.

Once Emmeline started she couldn't stop and within the hour this stranger knew the whole history of Isabella and Belle Isle. Here was the storybook princess at work once again. The gentleman and the little boy listened with intrigue. What a wonderful storyteller, he thought. He couldn't help but ask, "How do you know so much history about the island?" "Isabella Curwen was my papa's cousin, so she was family," Emmeline told him proudly. "So, your name is Curwen. Mine is Stenhouse. I have just shifted here so the area is new to me. We both like it here, don't we, son? Look at those beautiful trees on Belle Isle," he said. "No, my name is Christian. John Christian Curwen planted thousands of trees; he was well up in the horticulture world, as well as a very astute businessman, by all accounts," replied Emmeline. "But then they were both very wealthy, of course." With that the dog came bounding over with a shoe in his mouth. "Oh my goodness, Bow has stolen another shoe; we had better find out where he got that from. Come on, son, we must go now. Thank you for telling us the history of Belle Isle and, of course, Isabella. Do you come here often?" he asked. "Yes, this is my most favourite place of all. I come here to dream and of course to look across at the enchanted island." They both got up to leave. "Bye, lady," said the little boy. "I hope we meet again," said the father, and away they went.

Emmeline looked at them as they left and thought how

sad for the little boy to have lost his mother so young. But Stenhouse, she had heard that name before ... but where? She liked the father; he was friendly and he was a dreamer. It was only then she realised that they had not exchanged first names. She hoped they would meet again, but now she had better make her way back or Jane would start to worry.

Today was Papa's burial day. A large crowd from the village had gathered along with businessmen and the miners from Papa's collieries. Her uncles and their families were there. Jane and the groundsman stood with her as the procession was ready to move. She was going to be strong for Papa today; he would want her to be so. She looked around and out of the corner of her eye she caught the glance of a young man, a stranger, but one who held eye contact with her for a few seconds before looking away. Something stirred inside of her, a feeling unknown to her. She looked at him again and this time he smiled at her ... who was this stranger? They trudged up the hill, behind the horse and the carriage that carried Papa's coffin, for what seemed like a long time. The service was held at the burial site, then silence reigned as the coffin was lifted from the carriage and carried to the gravesite. It was time for Emmeline to say her final farewell to her beloved Papa, so she knelt down and put his favourite, a red rose, on his coffin as it was lowered into its final resting place. She stood and cried as she watched the men put the earth over the coffin.

Jane had arranged food and a cup of tea for everyone so they made their way down the hill to Emmeline's home. She spoke politely to those she knew, but there were so many strangers; they must have been from Papa's collieries. All the workers liked Mr Christian; he had seen to it they were treated well, and that so many had come to pay their respects spoke for itself. What was going to happen now that he was gone? This thought was on all the men's minds. Who would they be working for now? Not for the uncles; these were the last men they wanted to work for, as they put their profit before the men's wellbeing, and they expected their pound of flesh. No one treated their miners as well as Mr Christian did. He gave the men extras, when no one else did. This left everyone guessing as to what was going to happen. Not even Emmeline knew what was in her papa's will, or really what he owned. She thought her uncles partly owned the collieries, as they had spent a lot of time with Papa in his office when he was very ill. Everyone knew she was now the sole heiress to Mr Christian's estate, but Emmeline didn't know, as she was just the dreamer and the storyteller. She looked around to see if she could see the stranger again, but, alas, he was gone. Her uncles came up to her and asked if the solicitor had been in touch with her about her papa's will. She told them he was coming tomorrow morning at ten o'clock.

Now that everyone had gone home and there was just Jane and Emmeline sitting together, she asked Jane, "Do you know of someone called Thomas?" Jane looked at her and bent her head and looked at the floor. "Why do you ask, Miss Emmeline?" "Because Papa mentioned the name Thomas before he passed away," she said. It was now time to tell her about the scandal that hit town before Mr Christian met Miss Emmeline's mama. "A young lady had been staying in town and met Mr Christian. They had a short romance and there was talk of her leaving because she was with child. No one knew more than that, if indeed it was true! But a few years later a lady and a young lad came to visit your papa and they went into his office and closed the door. This was after your mama had passed away. When they left, I can remember your papa saying "Goodbye, Thomas." I have never mentioned this to anyone, as Mr Christian has been good to me and my family, so I don't gossip to anyone." "Do you think Papa was Thomas's papa?" asked Emmeline. "It's not my place to say," she said. "I work here and nothing leaves this home, it stays within these walls. I have moved my clothes into one of the spare rooms until you decide you want to be here on your own, then I will return to my lodgings." Emmeline was pleased Jane was staying, as she had never been on her own in this big home, but it was something she would have to get used to.

The next morning just before ten o'clock, Mr Edward Stenhouse arrived. So that was where she had heard that name before! She wondered if she should ask him if he had any relations living here. "Excuse me, Mr Stenhouse, do you have any family living in this area?" "Yes, a cousin has just moved here with his young son. Why do you ask?" he wanted to know. "It's just that I met them down by the lake a couple of days ago," said Emmeline.

"Now for the reading of your father's will. You probably don't realise, Miss Emmeline, that you are a very wealthy young lady. Everything of your father's was left to you, even the collieries. You are now responsible for the running of the collieries and all the men that work there." "But I thought my uncles owned part of the collieries," she interrupted. "No, your uncles wanted your father to sign them over to them when he was very ill, but he was concerned for the men's wellbeing. He said they should run themselves, as he had good men in charge of each department; that's why he has left them to you. He knew you wouldn't put profits first. They will report to you with any problems, and you only have to ask me and I can give advice, but the final say is ultimately yours. Your father left a healthy bank balance, so now you are in control of his whole estate. Just one last request: your father was afraid that his brothers might try to persuade you to let them run the collieries; he did not want this to happen, as the miners would lose a lot of the rights that have been given to them. Remember, I am available any time should you need me, this I promised your father." He then got up from his chair and tipped his hat to Emmeline and left.

It wasn't half an hour after he left that her uncles arrived. They asked her to come to her papa's office where they sat around his desk. "Now that your papa has gone, Emmeline, what is going to happen to the collieries?" they wanted to know, hoping they had been left to them to run. "Papa has left everything to me and he wants me to carry on with the colliery operations. He has asked his solicitor to guide me, but he has left good, reliable men in charge, so they should run themselves," she told them. "But you are only a girl, Emmeline, you know nothing about the collieries. Let us take them over and we will pay you a royalty. We know your papa was too soft with his men; we could double the output, as the miners need to be put in their place at times," they told her. She didn't want to upset them so said she would think about it for a week, but all the time she knew she would abide by her papa's wishes. She had a lot of thinking to do, as now Papa's estate was hers, so she could not go back to boarding school.

A few days later, Emmeline decided to ask Mr

Stenhouse to accompany her to the coal-pit so she could call a meeting with the men to lay to rest the rumours that were going around about Mr Christian's brothers taking over the collieries. There was unrest brewing. The miners were called to a meeting in the hall. Mr Stenhouse introduced Miss Emmeline, then she addressed the men: "Today I want you to know nothing will change at the collieries, they will carry on as usual. I am your new employer. Papa wanted me to tell you all he was very happy with your work ethic, so there will be no changes. I hope I can be as well liked as my papa." With this there was a roar from the miners; now it was all settled, they were able to carry on as normal. The rumours were quashed, there was no change in management. They would get on and please their new boss. Mr Stenhouse was very surprised by Miss Emmeline's courage to stand up and confront these men, and even better, she had won them over. Tomorrow she would hold a meeting with the charge hands and get an insight to each one's position and what was expected of them. She would take her papa's briefcase and notepad and write everything down so it was recorded. She was pleased with herself, Papa would be proud of her! Was this because of her papa's plea not to let the uncles take over that gave her the courage she needed? There would have been trouble and perhaps strikes if the men's extras were taken away.

Then she remembered she had to inform the uncles as to her decision about the collieries. She had barely put her foot in the door when they arrived and they were very angry. They had been to the collieries and tried to exert their authority but met with resistance because the new boss had been and spoken to the men. "Who has taken charge of the collieries?" they wanted to know. "I am their new boss. I held a meeting and they all know everything will remain the same. There will be no changes; that is the way Papa wanted it," she said in a stern voice. They told her it would not work, the miners needed someone in charge that would rule with an iron hand, and if her papa hadn't been so soft with them, the output of coal could have doubled; all the men had to do was work harder. This is exactly what her papa had told her would happen if they took over; it would be money first, then the men. This made her all the more determined to take control and find out how the collieries worked. Now the daydreaming was over; it was down to business!

5

Emmeline's Life Change!

Tonight, she would sit at her papa's desk and go through all the information she could on the collieries. She wanted to know how many men worked for her, how many men were in each shift, and exactly what they were paid. She would make her own files so she knew where to go to find things. It would take her a long time to know most things, but this was the start. As she was reading up on the collieries she was shocked to read the Whitehaven collieries were plagued with 'firedamp', or methane, and as the miners were expected to work at great depths, this was frightening. Because they worked at these depths, ventilation became a problem; in fact, it was critical, as an accumulation of gases precipitated explosions. She didn't want to lose any of her miners. As she read on she was upset to read that for some employers, the damage done

by an explosion to a colliery was more important than
the loss of life. This was barbaric; how could a destroyed
colliery mean more than men's lives? But there were
ruthless men in this business; all they wanted were the
profits at any cost! Her papa was different; he put the
safety of his men first and foremost and he was rewarded
for this. There had been no strikes or unrest in his
collieries, in fact men were lining up to come and work for
him, but because he treated the men right, no one left. The
men trusted and liked Mr Christian; that was seen by the
attendance at his burial.

Today Emmeline rode in the horse-drawn carriage to the
coal-pit with Mr Stenhouse to meet and address the
charge hands and to see if they wanted to ask her any
questions. She felt uncomfortable in his company as his
nervous twitch was a distraction. As much as she tried to
ignore it, it would not go away. Poor man, she thought, it
would be enough to put any fair maiden off. She didn't
think he would be married with that annoying habit! The
men gathered and listened to Emmeline as she addressed
them. She wanted them to know that first and foremost in
the collieries was safety. She valued each life that entered
the shafts and she wanted them to return safely, as she
knew the risks they were taking. She asked each man to
register his name and what section he was responsible for.
This would give her a greater understanding of what was
expected of the charge hands. It was most unusual for a
lady to be a boss, especially one so young and pretty, but as
long as it was run the same way Mr Christian ran it, there
would be no problems.

Emmeline decided to spend the rest of the morning at

the coal-pit and mix with some of the miners. She told Mr Stenhouse he could take his leave. "I don't think it is proper for a young lady to be mixing with miners," he said. "Thank you, Mr Stenhouse, you may take your leave," Emmeline told him politely. He slumped off and took his nervous twitch with him. She walked into the office and all the men stood as she came in. "Please be seated, I've just come to familiarise myself with Papa's business." She looked around and everything seemed to be tidy and workable. She selected an older man to explain what went on in each department. He walked with her and told her all she wanted to know. Suddenly a blast went off, which made Emmeline jump. "It's all right, Miss, this is the change of shift. The miners that started at midnight are now finishing their shift and a new batch of men will go down," he explained. "Please take me to meet the miners that have worked all night," she asked. "But, Miss, they will be blackened with coal dust," he protested. With this he took her over to the mine entrance where the miners were pulled up from great depths in a cage. As they climbed out of the cage she put her hand out and shook their hands. They were surprised; this had never happened before. All she could see were their eyes and their mouths, as the rest of them was black with the coal dust. How unhealthy for them, she thought.

As the last man came up she went to shake his hand and he gripped her hand hard. She looked at him and recognised the eyes; it was the young man who had smiled at her at Papa's burial. So, he was a miner! Emmeline looked at him for a moment and her heart started beating a little faster than usual. Who was this man? she wondered. As she looked down, she saw that her dress was covered in coal dust; it must have come off the miner's hands. "Sorry about your dress, Miss, it will be ruined," he told her politely. Emmeline blushed as he passed this comment, then he was gone. "Who was that young man?" she asked. "That is Ewan Thomas Fletcher, the strongest miner we have. He is only here for a short time as he is studying the lives of the miners, so wanted to experience the life they lead underground and the conditions they have to work in. You won't have a worry, Miss, your father ran the safest colliery here in the district; this will be in your favour," he told her.

Emmeline thanked her guide and decided to walk up the hill and breathe in some fresh air. What a terrible life these men have, thought Emmeline, but if they didn't have the collieries they would have no work therefore they couldn't provide for their families, so this was the only option for them. Not everyone had a privileged life like her and Isabella. She saw the work wagonette coming, so she hailed it down. The driver stopped and she climbed on. All the miners got up to give her their seat, so she thanked them and sat down on the front seat. Fancy their boss lady riding in the work wagonette with them; again this was a first. She was gaining their respect. As they pulled up at the drop-off point in town, the men waited until Emmeline dismounted. The first man off to see that she was safely down was Ewan Thomas Fletcher. "What a state you are in," he reminded her. "I'm not worried, Mr Fletcher, I've enjoyed meeting the men. Thank you for your kind words." And with that she held her head high and walked off. This left him deflated; he didn't mean to offend her, but how did she know his name?

Later that afternoon Emmeline took herself to her favourite spot by the lake. She hadn't been down for over a week, as other things had consumed her time. No place was as beautiful as her Belle Isle. The leaves were starting to turn colour on the trees, reminding her that autumn was descending upon the lake. Soon the evening mists would start rolling in giving the island a haunted look. Emmeline closed her eyes and it didn't take long for the dreaming to start.

"Hello, lady," a little voice interrupted her. She opened her eyes and here was the little boy she had seen on her last visit to the lake. He came and sat beside her. "Hello, little one, how are you today?" she asked. "Daddy is away along the lake, he will be here soon. He has been down two times but you haven't been here," he said innocently. "Oh, that's nice. Are you liking living here? Have you settled in?" she asked. "Yes, I love the lake. Sometimes it is angry and rough, but look at it now — there are no waves, it is peaceful." Emmeline was taken aback by his expression of her lake. What a dear wee soul, she thought.

Next thing up bounded a soggy wet dog, which decided to shake itself. Water flew everywhere wetting Emmeline and the little boy. "Get away and shake yourself," said an angry voice. "I'm so sorry he has wet you, I will put his lead on," said the little boy's father. "It's okay, no harm done," she answered. "I haven't seen you down here lately?" he enquired. "No, I have been busy at the colliery with the miners. How are you settling in?" Emmeline asked. "We love it here. I have just been offered a job as a teacher at the school. I'm really thrilled as it works in well with my son," he said. "I know your cousin Mr Stenhouse. He is my papa's solicitor," said Emmeline. "Edward is a clever man," he answered. "Is he married?" she asked. "He was for a short time, but apparently his wife left him for another man. It devastated him and he developed a nervous twitch." "That is so sad. I'm sorry but I don't even know your first name. I'm Emmeline," she said. "Pleased to meet you. I am Desmond," he said with a grin. "And I'm John," said the little boy, and with this they all laughed. "Isn't it interesting how a small town has so much history? If you hadn't told me about Belle Isle, I would never have known how important that island was. Townspeople can tell strangers so much about their local area, and the secrets that go unnoticed. Do you live near the lake?" Desmond asked. "Yes, I can see Lake Windermere from my home. Every time I look out the window the dreaming starts; it has been my whole life. But things have changed since Papa passed away; I spend so much time at the collieries now." Poor girl, thought Desmond, she must help out at the collieries, although she seems well educated.

The next morning Mr Stenhouse asked for Emmeline to come to his office. He was looking forward to seeing her again; she certainly had a mind of her own, and he was pleased how she handled herself at the meeting. He was most taken with her new-found ability, forgetting for a moment she was only sixteen. She made her way to his office and was asked to wait, Mr Stenhouse would be available shortly. She didn't have to wait long, "Hello, Miss Emmeline, please come through to my office," he asked of her. This was the first time she had been here. He pulled up a chair for her to sit down. "How are you coping? I hope you didn't meet with any problems at the coal-pit after I left you," he enquired. "No, the men were very polite. I met all the miners coming off the night shift and shook hands with them as they got out of the cage," she said. Mr Stenhouse was shocked; no young lady should be shaking hands with the miners who were covered in coal dust, it just wasn't right. "I ended up covered in coal dust myself but it didn't matter, as I rode home on the work wagonette with them." "Miss Emmeline, you are a young lady and an heiress, it is unheard of to be seen with the miners, but to ride home with them, that is ludicrous. You should have ridden home in a carriage. What were you thinking?" he scolded her. "Mr Stenhouse, I am no different to the miners; we all live in this town together. That my papa was wealthy makes no difference to me. The men are making money for me so I will mix with them," she said sternly. Poor Mr Stenhouse was put in his place. What a spirited young lady, but he was frightened this might lead to disaster. Would the workers take advantage of her generosity and her sex?

Mr Stenhouse was from the old stuffy English way of thinking. The workers were just that, workers; the upper class were way above the working class. This is where Emmeline belonged; she was wealthy, young and pretty, she should not even be near the collieries. Mr Christian ran the collieries from his home, only visiting when he needed to. He was very good to his miners, providing them with small extras for which they were grateful. But Emmeline, she was different to anybody he had ever known. In fact, she fascinated him, but this jolted his memory as to why he had asked her to come to his office today. "Miss Emmeline, your uncles have come to me with a proposal to lease your collieries. They think you are too young to run them, and they are worried, like myself, that the miners will take advantage of you because of your sex." "Well, Mr Stenhouse, you can forget you asked me this, because my answer is no. Papa told me what he wanted and I will see to his wishes," she replied. "My uncles are greedy; they work the miners to the bone and there is always unrest at their colliery. They lack empathy towards the miners; I will never treat my miners like they do." "But won't you even consider their proposal? They are offering you good money, and you wouldn't have to go near the collieries or indeed the miners ever again."

He thought this was a good offer, as he worried about her safety at the coal-pit. She was a little too familiar with the working class, and this was not seen as politically correct for a lady as wealthy as she was. She was expected to act more lady-like, not to greet the miners who were covered in coal dust; it made him shudder, which started off his twitches. Emmeline almost had to stop her smile turning to laughter as she saw him becoming more agitated and the twitches begin. "I'm sorry, Mr Stenhouse, my answer is still no. I like the miners; they are the ones who have made my father wealthy and now they work for me. I will continue to look after them."

He could see he was losing his battle with Emmeline, and his advice was not being heeded. He was told by the uncles there would be unrest among the miners as other bosses weren't offering their workers the extras that Emmeline's papa offered. This worried him. He could see if the uncles took over they would rule with an iron hand and would bring all the miners into line, thus taking the extras away from Emmeline's miners. Then it would be a level playing field. Mr Stenhouse was not at all sympathetic towards the working class; that was all they were ... working class. Now he would have to report back to the uncles on her decision. He knew they would be angry; they needed their niece's collieries, as the one they had was not as profitable.

Emmeline's papa had put in many years of hard work to acquire the land and establish the collieries. It was nigh on impossible to start from scratch today, so the only way to own a colliery was to buy an established one. Deep down in Mr Stenhouse's heart he admired Emmeline; her wealth was growing, but she didn't seem to grasp the position she was in. She could travel and buy what she wanted, but this didn't seem to register with her. He had looked at her spending but it was very little other than for personal use. What was she going to do with all her wealth? he wondered. Was he becoming attached to her? Surely not, she was just a child in his mind! At sixteen, you weren't meant to have sensual feelings; that was a no-no. He was a man who came across as a cold fish. He could wait a few years, then he might be interested. For him to take her away from the miners was to persuade her to sell to her uncles, but he would have to let it rest for now. "I am asking you not to visit the collieries again; it is not proper for you to be seen at the coal-pits," he told her. He had heard stories back about the pretty young boss; this was talk coming from the miners. "Mr Stenhouse, you will not give me orders. I will visit the collieries as I please. You are my papa's solicitor, not my minder," she reminded him.

Up until now he had protected her against her uncles, but as he became more infuriated with her, he was coming around to their way of thinking. She was classes above the miners and this is where he wanted her to remain. To lower herself to their standard was not at all proper for a lady of her standing. But to Emmeline there were no standards or rankings to her way of thinking. She only had to think back to Isabella, who chose John, the rich cousin, but to her way of thinking she chose the wrong man; she should have chosen Fletcher, who loved her.

Today she decided to go to the coal-pit to have a look at

the safety procedures to see that they were all up to date. She had arranged to meet the safety officer, who would explain what was required to keep the miners safe while at such depths. In 1816, thirty years earlier, Sir Humphry Davy tested a new 'safe lamp' in an area with the severest possible conditions, and that was in the collieries in the Whitehaven area, as they were notorious for the amount of 'firedamp', or methane, they produced, as well as the high fatality rate among miners. Also, the possibility of pit explosions could be predicted by studying barometric pressures; a 'falling glass' increased the chance of explosions. These measures were crucial to the collieries' safety. A new safety practice called 'coursing', or directing ventilation around the workings in order to remove still and poisonous gases, was being introduced. Emmeline wanted to make sure this procedure was being implemented in her collieries.

At this period in time in the mid-1800s there was no universal standard of safety, only industry-appointed impartial inspectors with limited authority. They then reported to the collieries' management with what they considered unsatisfactory. Consequently, some collieries initially escaped inspectors and continued to operate in an unsafe manner. Emmeline's papa had a policy not to employ women and children to work in his collieries. They were employed in other collieries where scruples were pretty crude. He could not bear the thought of children working underground and this was installed in Emmeline; no children were allowed anywhere near the coal-pits. Sometimes they were caught as they sneaked down to feed the horses that were plodding their way round and round the circular gin area to haul the tubs of coal from the bottom shafts.

6

Disaster at a Colliery

One night Emmeline was woken by a siren. This was the sound dreaded by everyone. This spelt disaster at one of the collieries. She quickly dressed and found her way to the village square where everyone gathered on hearing this warning. She saw Mr Stenhouse pull up with horse and carriage so ran over and asked him to take her to her coal-pit. Of course, he protested about her going, as this was no place for a young lady. She was worried for her miners so had to see they were safe.

As they reached the coal-pit there was nothing that looked like trouble. Emmeline jumped from the carriage before it was even stationary and ran into the office. "Is everybody safe?" she yelled. She was told there was a flood in her uncles' colliery. The pit was two miles under the sea and something had happened that led to the sea breaking in. Because no one survived, no one knew what had happened to cause this. One of the office men said, "Those poor miners were pushed to the limit. They were expected to go further under the sea to find seams of coal, all for greed." Emmeline was saddened by this, and it brought back to her what her papa had told her about her uncles. She would never give them the rights to her collieries. As she was standing in the office being given the terrible news, in rushed Mr Ewan Thomas Fletcher wanting to know if everything was okay at their collieries and were the men all safe. "I'm sorry, Miss Christian, I heard the siren so I had to come down," he said. "I thank you, Mr Fletcher. We all dread waking to the siren, but thankfully all our miners are safe, but we must spare a thought for those who have perished." "Whose colliery did this happen at?" he enquired. "Unfortunately, at my uncles' colliery. How did you get here?" she asked. "As soon as I heard the siren I dressed and started running." "You must come home with us," offered Emmeline. It was still dark.

They walked out of the office together and up to Mr Stenhouse's carriage. "Excuse me, Mr Stenhouse, we have a passenger to take back with us. Meet Mr Fletcher, he is a miner." Never before had a miner been invited to ride with him; he was aghast at the thought of a common miner taking a ride in his carriage. If it had been anyone else other than Miss Emmeline that had asked, he would have refused. As they were driving home she thanked Mr Fletcher for showing concern for the men. She told him it showed the comradeship among the miners, which made her proud. Mr Stenhouse cringed on hearing such heroic phrases being bestowed on a miner. Emmeline would have to be told how to contain her feelings towards the lower class. He would ask her to his office tomorrow. "Where do you live?" she asked. "I have a little cottage down by the lake in Marque Street," he said. "We will drop you off there," she said. Poor Mr Stenhouse; his patience was certainly being tested tonight. They pulled up in front of his home and Mr Fletcher alighted and thanked Mr Stenhouse for the ride. "I will see you tomorrow at the pit," she called to him.

As they drove away, Mr Stenhouse could not hold his peace until the morning. "You cannot go to the colliery today, it is not proper or safe. The men will be agitated over what has just happened. They will want answers. It is no place for a lady, especially with it being your uncles' colliery." "My uncles are not connected to my and Papa's collieries. That is why Papa didn't want them to get his; they are only in it for the money. Imagine those poor families without a breadwinner and children without a father. What if there were children in the shafts? There would mothers without their babies. Imagine that, Mr Stenhouse," replied an angry Emmeline. Thank goodness Papa didn't employ children.

It was only two years ago a law was brought in to protect the younger children; now they had to be ten years of age before they could work in the collieries. "Your charitable words are wasted on the miners. They are men who have no ambition; all they are any use for is to go underground and dig for coal," he said crossly. "Tell me, Mr Stenhouse, what do you burn to keep warm?" "I burn coal on my fires," he answered. "There you go, you would go cold if not for the miners. Please remember that," she said sternly. As he pulled up outside her home she alighted and thanked him coldly for taking her to the coal-pit. He noticed her tone of voice towards him. Yet she was more charitable towards Mr Fletcher and all he was, was a miner.

Was it because of his age and fine looks? he wondered as his twitch took over.

The next morning Emmeline asked her groundsman to take her back to the coal-pit. She would call a meeting with the men on the change-over of shifts, thus both shifts would be present. It would hold the workings up for an hour, but she wanted to speak to all the men. She waited at the office until the change-over, then asked all the men to gather in the yard. Some were black with coal dust, while others were just going to start their shift. "You will all have heard what happened last night; we must mourn for those lives that were lost. I want to give you an assurance that all safety procedures are in place in my collieries, but accidents do happen, this we must be mindful of. The collieries will shut down so you can all attend a memorial service when it is held. Your pay will continue, no one will lose money. I will inform you when the service is to be held and the hours the collieries will be shut down. Thank you, everyone." A roar of appreciation was expressed by her men. They held the upmost respect for her papa, now it was filtering on to her. At that moment a miner came up and stood by Emmeline. "On behalf of all the miners at Miss Christian's collieries, we wish to express our gratitude for her concern for her men and their safety." This was endorsed by cheering and clapping. Emmeline knew that voice; it belonged to Mr Ewan Thomas Fletcher. She personally thanked him for his kind words. His reply was: "You are highly thought of by the men. They were worried when Mr Christian passed away that your uncles were going to run the collieries. Imagine the uproar now. We thank you, Miss Emmeline." Then he was gone. She felt disappointed as she wanted to thank him again for arriving at the coal-pit earlier that morning.

There was a lot of speculation circling about the tragedy at the colliery. Twenty-five men and five young boys had lost their lives. The boys had been working up front in the shaft. Because they were smaller in stature, they were made to crawl along and pick and shovel the way forward. Then the men would follow. This was a terrible tragedy, but it was not the first and it would not be the last.

Families gathered in the village square all sobbing, as this was something they had experienced many times. The lucky ones still had their breadwinners, but they shared their heartache with others. Now the colliery would be shut down as the sea had flooded through it. This meant no work for the remaining miners; how were they going to survive? Were her uncles going to compensate the families? The uncles' future wealth had gone; would they try to acquire her collieries again? Because of the poor return from the colliery, the miners were pushed to the limit by her uncles, going under the sea-bed, which was always in imminent danger of flooding. But the miners had no other option other than to do what was asked of them, otherwise how were they going to feed their families?

Mr Stenhouse had asked Miss Emmeline to come to his office. It had been brought to his attention that she had offered her men time off work to attend the memorial service for the lost men, and they were still to get paid. "Do you think that is wise?" he asked. She let him know that if that was what she decided, then it would be happening. "It is something I feel deeply about, in fact it is important that everyone share in the village grief." "But you are creating dissatisfaction among the other colliery bosses. The men are demanding the same conditions that you are offering to your men. Can you not see this could lead to trouble?" he asked. "I care for my men, they come first before profit, but that is not so with many of the bosses, therefore their problems are not mine. What will become of the families who have lost their breadwinners? I am a woman; it's a pity more collieries aren't run by women, then lives would matter," she told him. Poor Mr Stenhouse, he was getting nowhere. He was one man who showed very little sympathy for the working class. He was only trying to protect Miss Emmeline but his mannerism was that of the stuffy upper-class English. He found himself more and more attracted to this headstrong young lady, but he didn't know how to deal with these feelings. To Emmeline he was just a middle-aged uninteresting man. The difference in ages was nineteen years, which was not frowned upon, as many upper-class men married much younger ladies. This was even encouraged by families, if they held positions or were wealthy. But this was not to be so with Emmeline as she was a free spirit, a dreamer!

The service for the lost men would be held in the village square on Thursday afternoon. Emmeline went down to the coal-pit and put notices up for the men to say the collieries would close on Thursday at twelve noon and reopen at noon on Friday. This would give them time to mourn for their fellow worker-mates who had perished out to sea. She wanted to do something for the widows and children who were left without husbands and fathers, so she would put together a food parcel for each family. It wasn't a lot but it would be a help. She hadn't seen her uncles since the tragedy but neither had anyone else. The miners that were left were angry, as they had no prospect of work.

Emmeline held a meeting with her charge hands and asked for Mr Fletcher to be there, to see if they could create work for some of these men. Mr Fletcher came up with an idea: "Miss Emmeline, we have half a dozen men who are thinking about retiring; perhaps if you offered them a severance pay, this would open up vacancies for younger family men." Emmeline thought this was an excellent idea and would take it back to Mr Stenhouse. "Thank you, Mr Fletcher, I agree we must try to look after the younger men with families, they are our future. If a severance pay is what is needed to help these men retire, then that is what I will offer them. They deserve retirement after all those years in the collieries." She knew their life expectancy was not great, as the coal dust had ruined their lungs. "Thank you for your time." As she was about to leave, Mr Fletcher stopped her. "Excuse me, but I would like to say you have been very fair to the men, and they appreciate all you have done for them." "I will always look after the miners; they have made my family wealthy, so I feel I owe them. Would you please call at my home just before the service tomorrow, as I have food parcels for the families who have lost their men? We will take them to the service and distribute them," she said. "Certainly, Miss Christian, that will be a pleasure," he answered. As she left the coal-pit, her heart was racing; was it Mr Fletcher that did this to her? Each time she had been in his company, this had happened. She did think he was a very strong, handsome young man. He seemed to take the position of leadership when speaking on behalf of the men.

Emmeline made her way to Mr Stenhouse's office to talk about severance pay. She was quite relieved when he agreed with her, and said he would look into it. "We will deal with this now. You come to me with what you think is a fair amount for these men to retire on, so they can enjoy the time they have left." As soon as this was worked out she could go to the men with an offer. Mr Stenhouse had decided that it was better to stay on-side with her, as the collieries were running favourably and her wealth was building nicely. "I will accompany you to the service tomorrow, Miss Emmeline," he stated. "Thank you, Mr Stenhouse, but Mr Fletcher is coming to help me with the food parcels for the families who have lost their men." This was a real blow for him. What was a miner doing getting involved with Miss Emmeline? Was he after her money? He had to admit, he was certainly a fine specimen of a man; had she realised this? He couldn't bear to think of anyone else taking her fancy. He had come to look upon Miss Emmeline as his ward and his future sweetheart. But she was still so young; she was just a girl, one who wouldn't know her feelings. She still had a few years before she started to show any interest in men ... really, Mr Stenhouse!

Emmeline contacted her uncles to get the names of the men and boys who had lost their lives. When they knew she was giving food parcels to the widows, they could not believe her kindness. It was a good look for them although it was coming from their niece, but it would help them save face. They had lost all their investment when the colliery was swamped with sea water. Now it was important that they try to secure Emmeline's collieries; they could never afford to buy them but they could go back with a good offer to lease them. Today was the day of the combined service for the men and boys; no bodies had been recovered from the sea. The towns of Bowness and Whitehaven and the surrounding districts were in mourning. These towns had been designed to attract miners and their families to work the collieries; it needed the men. Some of the colliery bosses owned houses in the town so they offered homes to their workers, but then they were tied to them. If they didn't like the working conditions in the collieries they couldn't leave, because otherwise they would have to get out of their homes, leaving them with nowhere to go.

All the people were gathering in the village square. Emmeline heard the front door bell ringing and went to invite Mr Fletcher in to the parlour where the food parcels were. She was quite shocked to see him all dressed up; my goodness, he did look handsome. His cheerful smile and strong voice set her heart racing once again. "What a stately home, Miss Emmeline. Oh, you have views of the lake. There is something about the lake — it has so many moods," he said. "Yes, it is my favourite place of all. I sit by it and dream a lot. Belle Isle is my enchanted isle. I know the whole history of Isabella, who the island was named after, ..." Then she had to stop herself rambling on.

"Time we were organised, as the service will be starting without us," he commented. She gathered up the food parcels and as she was handing them to him their hands touched and she left her hand touching his for a few seconds before taking it away. Never before had she done anything like this, and she was annoyed with herself for displaying an emotional gesture to a man she hardly knew. Should she apologise or just let it pass? "Oh, I'm sorry, Mr Fletcher," she apologised. "Don't worry, Miss Emmeline, you can do it again any time," he answered with a grin, one that again melted her heart. This has to stop! she told herself.

They walked down to the square with the parcels. Emmeline had previously spoken with the minister, so he was going to ask the families who had lost a loved one to meet her after the service. She asked Mr Fletcher if he would be with her as she gave out the food parcels; this he agreed to. The service was very moving and touched everyone in the village square, as this was not the first time, but it was the way of life for the miners and their families; they lived on the brink of disaster every day. Mr Edward Stenhouse had come down to the square and was standing among the crowd when he saw Miss Emmeline standing with Mr Fletcher and they seemed to be engaged in deep conversation. Why would she be seen in public with a miner? She was the wealthiest young woman in all of Windermere and Whitehaven. How degrading, he thought to himself, but he knew she was just sixteen years of age, one who was too young to realise her position in life. When she reached eighteen, he would make known his feelings for her. After all, she was his ward ... in his mind only.

As the miners' families met with Emmeline, she said how sorry she was and handed them all a parcel for which they were most grateful. Any help in this situation was welcomed. She promised to visit them and see how they were managing. In all it was a sad day, the first that she had attended, and she hoped it would be the last. She was very disappointed not to see her uncles there, as she felt it was their duty to grieve with the townspeople.

While talking to Mr Fletcher, she felt a tug on her dress and looked down to see the little boy she had met at the lake front. "Hi, Miss Emmeline," he said. "Hello, little John, where is your father?" she asked. "There he is," he said proudly as he pointed to him. "Hi, Emmeline, what a sad day for the townspeople today," he said. "Desmond, please meet Mr Fletcher. He has helped me with parcels for the miners' widows; he works at the collieries." "Pleased to meet you, Mr Fletcher," answered Desmond. Who is this man that calls Miss Emmeline by her first name? he wondered. As Emmeline and Desmond started talking, he bade them farewell and left. Emmeline was sad, as she hadn't had time to thank him.

Emmeline and Desmond chatted away; she liked him and found him so easy to talk to, probably because they were both dreamers. While they were talking, Mr Stenhouse appeared and greeted his cousin. "Emmeline and I met down by the lake one day," Desmond told him. Edward looked on in shock horror at his cousin addressing Miss Emmeline by her first name without the proper formalities. "Desmond, this is Miss Emmeline Christian. She owns two big collieries here and a lot of these men work for her." "Oh, I'm sorry, I didn't know that. I thought she must have worked in the office at the colliery," he said apologetically. "It's all right, Desmond, we are friends; just keep calling me Emmeline." This put a different light on things, as he thought she was just an ordinary person like himself.

"That was good of you to help the widows in their hour of need; they will think kindly of you," said Mr Stenhouse. He was so stuffy in his thinking and this annoyed her. Why did he have to assert his authority over his own cousin? It was irrelevant to her if people called her Miss Emmeline or merely Emmeline. Formalities were not a big thing with her. "Miss Emmeline, did you see the lake this morning? It was very angry," little John said. "No, I didn't, but perhaps it was sad for the miners who lost their lives," she said. "Yes, that is probably why," he answered. She was taken with his interest in the moods of the lake. Mr Stenhouse didn't pay much attention to the little boy. "Desmond, I would like to see you in my office when it next suits you," he said. With this, he bid his farewells and left.

"I'm sorry I didn't address you properly, but I didn't know your status," apologised Desmond. "You are my friend and I told you my name; just call me Emmeline. Your cousin is quite stuffy. He doesn't approve of my going to the collieries and mixing with the miners, but they are the men who keep my collieries going; I need them. I am no better than them, but he promised my papa that he would protect me. He is very upper-class English, a little pompous. How do you find him?" she asked. "Oh, Edward and I are so different. He always considered himself above the working class; he was an only child so had the top education bestowed on him at the best schools. We tolerate him. We were surprised when he married but it didn't last, sadly; he is such an emotionless person." "Yes, I agree. I would like to say something that would shock him just to see his expression change," said Emmeline. "Where do you live, Miss Emmeline?" asked little John. "See that big home just over there at the foot of the hill? That is my home." "Daddy and I walked past there yesterday, and he said someone posh must live there, it is so big. So you must the posh person." Both Emmeline and Desmond burst out laughing, as it sounded so innocent coming from the mouth of a child. "Would you like to come and see my home?" she asked. "Yes, please!"

With this they left the village square and walked to her home. Just before they entered, little John stood and looked at the stately home. He was bewildered by the sheer size of it. As they entered into the hallway there were so many doors. "Come, let us go to my favourite room, the drawing room, and I will show you a painting of the lady who owned Belle Isle," she said. They were amazed at the size of the painting and how beautiful Isabella was. Emmeline pulled up a chair for each of them to sit on and gaze at the painting. "This is beautiful, Emmeline. No wonder you wanted to find out the history on this lady. To think she is a family member, how wonderful! You are so lucky to have such knowledge, you should have been a teacher," he said. "All I ever wanted to be was a writer. I don't have the time to write or dream since Papa passed away, as I am busy with the collieries. My uncles wanted to take them over but Papa told me not to let them, as they are in it for the profit, not for the men's wellbeing. I treat the miners with respect and that is what I earn back from them," she said, realising that she had never spoken so freely with anyone except her papa. She apologised for gabbling on. "Don't apologise, Emmeline, you are a very interesting person. I enjoy our time together," he replied. "Yes, Miss Emmeline, you make Daddy and me happy," said a little voice from a big chair. It was time for them to leave and as they said their goodbyes, Desmond took her hand and thanked her. She did not feel the same feeling that Mr Fletcher generated when their hands touched. She enjoyed her time with Desmond and his little boy. They shared the same values as she did; it was an easy friendship, and she was still the storyteller.

Emmeline, try as she did, couldn't get Mr Ewan Thomas Fletcher off her mind; he was always there lingering in the background. Today she decided she wanted to see him again so she asked the groundsman to take her in the horse-drawn carriage to the coal-pit. She had studied up about the collieries and with each day she learned a little more. This week Mr Fletcher was on night shift so would be coming up in the cage about 12.10pm. She would be there again today to greet the miners, so when the siren went, she made her way over. She spoke with the miners that were waiting to go down and wished them a safe return. As the night-shift workers surfaced, she spoke with each one of them. The last miner up was the strongest man, Mr Fletcher. "I didn't get time to thank you for your help the other day, you were gone before I realised," she said. "Oh, you had friends to talk to, I didn't want to be a bother," he replied. "I would like you to come to my home so we can talk about the collieries, as I have some questions I would like to ask you. Would tomorrow night suit after you have slept?" asked Emmeline. He said he would come about 9.30pm if that wasn't too late, then he would just go straight to work at midnight.

Meanwhile, Desmond called in to his cousin Mr Stenhouse's office as was requested. He didn't know why he had been asked to call but he would soon find out. "Sit down, Desmond. The purpose of my invite to you is about Miss Emmeline. I was upset when you addressed her in public without the formalities. She is a very wealthy young lady; she is an heiress to a vast fortune and should be addressed accordingly. I ask that in future that you call her Miss Emmeline as a show of respect." Desmond was taken by surprise at his cousin's reasoning. He and Emmeline were friends on an equal level, she had told him that; they enjoyed each other's company, wealth was never on his mind. He would tell Edward this. "I'm sorry, Edward, but Emmeline and I are friends, there is no class distinction separating us, and I will continue to call her Emmeline as she has requested of me. John and I spent the afternoon with her at her home; the three of us get on really well together, we have a lot in common," Desmond told him in earnest.

Did he detect a hint of jealously from his cousin, that he had not been asked to drop the formalities? Emmeline was certainly right about his stuffiness, it was there all right;

he definitely considered himself upper class. Did he have dibs on her? Her money and title were a certain draw-card for Edward; it would put him right up there in society, up where he belonged ... or longed to be? Desmond asked if that was all, then took his leave. Poor Mr Stenhouse, he was so upset to learn his cousin had spent an afternoon with Miss Emmeline at her home. What did they have in common? he wondered. He was only a schoolteacher, a dreamer, one without much ambition. What was Miss Emmeline thinking of? She was but a child. He hoped she wasn't going to mix with common people and ignore her own class. He would have to teach her to be more upper class. Perhaps he could ask her out to a business meeting where she would meet people of her own status — rich people, ones that mattered. He would try this.

7

Mr Ewan Thomas Fletcher

Emmeline sat and watched the clock tick over; let it be 9.30pm soon, she prayed. She was so excited and that feeling had come back; there were butterflies in her stomach. But he wasn't even there yet. Why was this happening to her now? Was it just the thought of him? Poor Emmeline, she struggled with these strange things happening in her body. Was this how Isabella felt when she met her cousins? Suddenly she was brought back to reality when Jane announced she had a visitor. She adjusted her dress and touched her braids, then went to greet Mr Fletcher. She invited him into the drawing room. As soon as she saw him she melted; his smiling eyes seemed to dance and play tricks with her. Although he had been to her home before, he hadn't been in the drawing room.

"This is a lovely room. Is that your mother in the painting? You both look alike," he said. "She is quite beautiful." Emmeline could not believe what she had just heard; fancy being likened to her heroine, and to be told she was beautiful. Did this mean she was beautiful too? "No, Mr Fletcher, that is not my mother, that is Isabella Curwen. She owned Belle Isle, the largest island in the lake." "Yes, I know about her. I think I read it; no, it was my mother who told me about her. What an intriguing story," he acknowledged. "Tell me, why are you working at the colliery?" she asked. "I am doing a thesis on the miners, their lives and the conditions they are expected to work under. This is the third colliery I have worked in. I am interested in the safety aspects of each colliery, and how well the miners are treated. It has been an interesting experience. Some bosses treat their miners as if they mean nothing; yours has been an exemplary model of how all collieries should be run. Your safety is excellent, you treat your miners with respect and that is shown in the respect they have shown your father and now yourself. You have had no unrest or strikes; that speaks for itself."

"Just before my papa passed away he asked me to run the collieries and look after the miners; he didn't want my uncles to take over the running of his collieries. Thank goodness I listened to him, now that I have seen what happens in collieries where the men are pushed to the limit. Those poor men and boys that perished, how sad. I hope I never have such a tragedy in my collieries, but I know things do go wrong," stated Emmeline. He told her that she was a kind person and certainly caring like her father. "All the men are talking about their pretty young boss and they feel as proud of you as I do." The colour flushed up in Emmeline's cheeks when she heard this. She thanked him for his compliment. She then asked him if he had spoken to the older men about severance pay. "They said they would be only too happy to stand down and let the younger men have the work so they could support their families. It is up to you now to negotiate with them from here on," he said. She thanked him and offered him a cup of tea before he left for work.

Jane brought the tea through to the drawing room. "Tell me about yourself, Mr Fletcher. Where do you come from?" asked Emmeline. He replied: "Could we please drop the Mr Fletcher and just call me Ewan? I lived not far from here with my mother, then when she remarried we shifted away to Cockermouth where my stepfather worked. They went on to have three children; they are much younger than me, but we all get on well together. My mother didn't want me to be a miner so she had some money put away for my education and I went on to university. I was always interested in the collieries, thus my thesis. I hope to write a book one day on my findings. From experience, I would hate to have to wake up each morning and know that for the rest of my life I was going to be working underground in among the coal dust. But it has amazed me how accepting the miners are. They are grateful for having a job and being able to provide for their families. To me, that is gratitude at its highest level! They are such humble beings. I admire the way you go to the coal-pit and mix with the miners. It gives them hope in their hearts; I have heard them talking. Keep up the good work!"

"I have enjoyed our talk, Ewan. Perhaps we could

continue another day?" Emmeline asked of him. "That would be fine by me, Miss Emmeline," he said. "I hope I see you at the coal-pit in the next few days!" He took his leave so he could catch the workers' wagonette that left from the square. As he was leaving Emmeline's just before midnight, Mr Stenhouse was walking back from a meeting and he witnessed Mr Fletcher in Miss Emmeline's driveway. He could not believe what he had just seen. What would Mr Fletcher be doing at her place at that hour of night? Was he a Peeping Tom? How would he handle this? It could not go on. Emmeline was just a child; to have someone peeping on her, this had to be stopped before it got out of hand.

The next morning, Mr Stenhouse paid Miss Emmeline a visit. He asked her if she drew her drapes at night, did she lock her doors and was Jane still living there with her? Did she hear any noises around her home last night? "Why are you asking me all these questions, Mr Stenhouse?" she asked. "When I was walking home from a meeting last night about midnight, I saw a man leaving your driveway," he said. Emmeline laughed. "That was Ewan leaving for his shift; he had been visiting me."

Ewan — since when was Mr Fletcher known as Ewan? What would he and Emmeline be doing to that hour of night? "Miss Emmeline, it is improper for you to be entertaining men at your home at that hour of night, you are a child. Your father would not have approved," he scolded her. "I am seventeen next week, Mr Stenhouse, I am not a child any more. My mama married my papa when she was eighteen." For this Mr Stenhouse had no answer; he just stood there bewildered. If he was not going to get through to her, he would take it upon himself to deal with Mr Fletcher. He was just a miner, he would only be hanging around to better himself. This was not going to happen ... he would see to this!

"While you are here, Mr Stenhouse, have you worked out a severance pay for the men who are going to retire?" she asked. "Yes, I have them with me," and he produced a wage sheet with the amounts on. Emmeline looked at them; it didn't seem enough as it would be the last amount of money they ever got to live on. "I want you to double that amount," she said. "But they are just miners, they don't need much money," he answered. "They need the same as you and me, Mr Stenhouse. They are people just like us. Please do as I ask. I will be around just before twelve o'clock to pick them up."

He had no answer to any of this so he slumped away with his nervous twitch; she knew when she had upset him, as his twitch got worse. He is so righteous, but that will not go down with me, she said to herself. Perhaps this was because she looked at life from a young, fresh perspective. He was definitely old school, she thought, but would she change him or break him? As he left, he had never felt so humiliated before in his life. This was a first, and it wouldn't be the last! Miss Emmeline was getting at him. The angrier he became, the more she reached his heart. Why was she doing this to him? She was hurting him. Was it because he realised he had feelings for her? Were they becoming stronger? She was like a naughty child.

Just before lunch, Emmeline called at his office to pick up the men's severance pay. He noticed there was something different about her, then he realised it was her hair. She had taken out her braids and let her hair down. Surely, she wasn't going to the coal-pit looking like that? he thought. He couldn't hold his tongue. "You look nice today, Miss Emmeline. Surely you are not going to the coal-pit?" "Indeed I am, Mr Stenhouse, I'm on my way right now." "Can I take you down?" he asked. He wanted to be there to protect her from the miners, as in his mind they would be talking about her in an inappropriate manner. "No, thank you, I have a ride," she let him know. This added insult to his earlier wound. After lunch he would take his horse and carriage to the coal-pit to see no harm had come to her.

Emmeline's groundsman took her down, and she would wait until the nightshift finished at 12.15pm and meet Ewan so he could introduce her to the men that were going to receive their severance pay. As soon as she heard the blast she went over to where the cage brought the men up. Ewan was the last man up; he stayed and made sure everyone went up safely, then it was his turn. When he saw Emmeline, he thought she looked so nice today. Covered in coal dust, he went over to her and called the men's names out that she had to meet, and asked them to come forward. "Meet Miss Emmeline, she will take you to the lunchroom and talk with you," he said. She thanked Ewan and asked the men to come with her.

They sat down around a table and she asked their names and how long they had worked at the colliery. They told her they had been miners all their working lives. "Are you sure you are ready to take your severance pay?" she asked them. All six agreed to call it a day and make way for the younger family men. Emmeline told them they could finish at the end of the pay week. She gave them their severance pay envelopes and an extra ten pounds in cash for their long service. When they opened their pay packets and saw the amount, tears formed in their eyes. She had been very generous and for this they were very grateful. "Thank you, Miss Emmeline, you are so kind."

As she was about to leave the building, someone shouted that there was a scuffle in the yard. She rushed out to see Mr Stenhouse and Ewan shoving each other, so she went over to see what was happening. All the men had gathered around cheering. "What is going on?" Emmeline asked. "Mr Stenhouse threatened me if I ever went near your home again. I told him to mind his own business," answered Ewan. The men yelled in agreeance. "Mr Stenhouse, please leave immediately," she said diplomatically, not wanting things to escalate, or make a fool of him in front of the miners. She noticed he had coal dust on his hands where he had shoved Ewan. That would be a first, she thought. Then she saw his trademark twitches in action as he walked away. "I'm sorry about that, Ewan," she said. The men all cheered. She walked away to where her groundsman was waiting and climbed into the carriage, and away they went.

What was she going to do about Mr Stenhouse? He was overreacting and trying to control who she saw. She asked to be dropped off at his office so she could get this sorted. He was upset with himself for causing a scene at Miss Emmeline's workplace, and having been asked to leave. How was he ever going to be able to face her again, but here she was! Before she could say anything Mr Stenhouse spoke: "I'm very sorry, Miss Emmeline, for my earlier conduct. I don't know what came over me; I will control myself in future," he said meaningfully. Deep down he had worked out why he reacted in this manner — he was jealous, but he couldn't tell her. He was totally embarrassed with himself; nothing like this had ever happened to him, but then he had never met anyone like her before. He would have to take control of himself! "You are a good man, Mr Stenhouse, but I am old enough to make my own decisions. I know Papa asked you to look after me, but that only related to business, not my private life. We will leave it at that," and she reached out to shake his hand in a friendly gesture. He put his hand across his desk and held her delicate hand; it felt so soft and warm. He wanted to bend down and kiss it, but that would not be proper at this time, when he had behaved so badly. "Thank you, Miss Emmeline, I am deeply sorry. It will never happen again," he promised her. She said her goodbyes and left his office, pleased that there wasn't a confrontation, as she didn't want to fall out with him; he was her business adviser, and a decent man. She was slowly warming to him and his twitches; he meant well. She read nothing else into this incident, but this was her innocent mind!

8

Filling the Vacant Positions at the Colliery

Now it was time for Emmeline to think about interviewing new miners for the six positions that were going to be vacant at the end of the week, plus three new ones they had created. She had held a meeting with the charge hands and they were in agreeance that they could take an extra three men to help the situation that had arisen from her uncles' colliery disaster. In fact, another vacancy had arisen as the office charge hand had asked for time off as he wasn't well, and he was told by his doctor the only way he was going to get better was to give up work for a few months. Emmeline thought she would ask Ewan if he wanted the position, as it would allow him to get experience in another field. This would rescue him from having to work among the coal dust; it would be much healthier for him, and give him more time to do his thesis. She would leave a message for him to come to her home tonight before his shift started at midnight.

She had put up a letter on the village notice board about the vacancies and for the miners to pick up a form at the coal-pit and fill it out as best they could, as many had never attended school. They had gone straight to the collieries to work to help support their families. She would give first options to the miners who were affected by her uncles' colliery closure, ones with families to feed. Ewan would probably know some of them, as the miners were a close-knit bunch. They talked loosely among themselves, so if he could pass on any information it would be helpful. She did so want to see him again. Emmeline did wonder how old he was; it was probably on his work record at the office, and she would have a look tomorrow when she went down to interview the men.

Jane came in with an envelope for Emmeline, which had just been delivered. When she opened it, there was a letter from Desmond wanting to know if she would like to row out to Belle Isle with him and little John on Sunday, if the lake was calm. They could have a picnic. She was so excited; she had always wanted to do this, but she had no one to go with. Later tomorrow she would go down to her favourite spot by the lake in hope of seeing Desmond, to let him know she would love to go. Emmeline liked Desmond and little John; they got on well together, it was if they were a family.

Emmeline went to the drawing room to curl up in her

favourite chair and gaze at Isabella while she waited for Ewan to arrive. She had let part of her braid out so a loose piece of hair fell down around her shoulders just to add a more feminine look. She didn't need any colouring on her cheeks as that happened the moment she set eyes on him. As she was sitting there, her thoughts went back to Isabella and her suitors, her two cousins. Their lives had matched up until now, but the only two cousins she knew were not family, they were Desmond and Mr Stenhouse. Was this a sign? she wondered. But Mr Stenhouse was too old and he was stuffy and had a twitch. Then she suddenly had a thought: why was he trying to keep Ewan away? Did he like her? ... Surely not! She liked Desmond, but what did all this mean? She knew her future ... but what was happening? This wasn't how it was meant to be.

"Emmeline, you have a visitor," announced Jane. She showed him through to the drawing room. She jumped out of her chair to greet Ewan. Gosh, he is such a strong-built young man, she thought to herself. With that, the colour flowed into her cheeks and she felt flushed. "You look pretty tonight, Miss Emmeline, and such rosy cheeks," he said smiling. Poor Emmeline, she had never felt so helpless; she just stood there and stared at him. "It's all right, I'm not going to bite you," he said. "Oh, I'm so sorry, forgive me, please sit down," invited an embarrassed Emmeline. "Ewan, one of my office charge hands is taking time off on his doctor's orders, as he is not well. I wondered if you would like his position, as I have to replace him. Perhaps it would give you more time to work on your thesis?" "I enjoy working with the miners and as my time is running out here, it would allow me to get bookwork experience. Yes, thank you, Miss Emmeline, I would like that," he answered.

What did he mean his time was running out? Surely he wasn't going to another colliery; how would she see him if he moved away? She dared not ask him, as she didn't want to know the answer. "Do you know any of the men that worked for my uncles who would be applying for a job at my collieries?" she asked him. He said he knew some of them and most were good men but there were a couple of narks among them. He didn't know who they were, but had heard the men talking. For their own safety, the miners would not mention names. She thanked him for his information. He agreed to have a cup of tea before leaving for work.

They chatted away and in her excitement, she mentioned she would be seventeen next week. "What will you be doing for your birthday?" he asked. She told him she had nothing planned; just she and Jane would be at home. "I'll come around and take you to supper. You have to celebrate your seventeenth birthday, it is very important. I can remember my seventeenth, that was about eight years ago now, but I still have good memories. I was much wilder back then," he said laughing. This was when Emmeline's heart started racing just seeing those smiling eyes light up; it was enough to wish he would take her in his arms.

Each time she met him she became more aware that something was happening inside of her. Could she talk about it with Jane, would she understand? Was this how Isabella felt when she eloped with John Christian? Was she falling in love? She wished she could talk to the girls back at boarding school, they would be able to tell her what to do. If only Papa was here to talk to, he would understand ... but alas, he was not! "Tell me the date of your birthday and I will come for you, as I will be on night shift," he asked. She told him it was on Tuesday, so arrangements were made. "I have to go now to catch the wagonette in the square, otherwise I will have to run to the coal-pit," he said. Emmeline stood up and walked to the front entrance with him; she so wanted to take his hand in hers but it was not the right thing to do. She said goodbye to him and ran back into the drawing room and burst into tears.

This was where Jane found her when she came to pick up the empty cups. "What is wrong, Miss Emmeline?" she asked kindly. "I think I am falling in love with Ewan," she answered. "That is a perfectly natural thing to happen, everyone falls in love. For some people it happens more than once, but we all start somewhere and this is where you are starting. He seems a nice young man but he won't be the last man you fall in love with," she said. What did she mean? Emmeline asked herself. I will only love one man like Isabella did.

Today was interview day with the miners so she asked her groundsman to take her in her carriage to the coal-pit. Emmeline set up a desk so she could interview each man. Twenty-five men had put their names forward, some wanting to change collieries to come and work where they would be better looked after than where they presently worked. She had made up her mind that the miners out of work from her uncles' colliery would be given first consideration. She had nine positions as well as Ewan's, as he was taking the office job offered to him. After talking to all the men, she chose young family men, all from her uncles' colliery, due to the disaster which left them without employment through no fault of their own. Emmeline did remember that Ewan had mentioned that there were a couple of narks among them but hopefully she had made the right selection with the miners she had chosen. The men were to start the following Wednesday on their given shifts, as that was the start of a new pay week. She handed the men's details on to the office charge who would file them away. Emmeline didn't see Ewan at the coal-pit today and really missed him. It was going to be different when he took his new job; she would see more of him.

9

A Visit to Belle Isle

Tomorrow was the big day she was really looking forward to. She, Desmond and little John were going to row out to Belle Isle just like Papa said her mama had done. But today she would help Jane put together a picnic basket so they wouldn't go hungry, especially little John. They cooked some potted beef and Jane made a crusty bread and baked a sweet cake. The lake was calm today and the weather was looking good for tomorrow. As she lay in bed that night, her head was all over the place. At last she was going to set foot on her favourite place of all, Belle Isle, her enchanted island. Of course, she would have to help Desmond row the boat, but first he would have to teach her as she hadn't used an oar before. It was all going to be such fun. They would sit under the beautiful trees and have a picnic and she would feel closer to her heroine.

When she woke this morning the first thing she did was check on the lake; it was calm, there wasn't a ripple on it anywhere. Jane helped Emmeline put everything into the basket, then they said their goodbyes and she made her way down to the lake. She could see Desmond rowing the boat to their meeting place and little John was waving madly at her. She waited until Desmond jumped out of the boat and came ashore and lifted the picnic basket, which he took back to the boat. Then he came back for Emmeline. He told her to jump up on his back and he would piggyback her to the boat. She had never been this close bodywise to any man, but she did as she was told. She put her arms around his neck and wrapped her legs around his waist, and held on tightly so she didn't end up in the water. "I'm so excited, Miss Emmeline, this is going to be a real adventure," said little John.

Once they were settled in their respective seats, Desmond took the oars and started rowing. Emmeline asked if she could help. "I may need a spell later on," he answered with a grin. Little John and Emmeline looked over the side of the boat to see who was first to see a fish, and it wasn't long before the first one was spotted by little John. They could see the pebbles on the lake bottom as the water was transparently clear, but as they got into deeper waters the bottom disappeared and the water became darker.

She hadn't taken much notice of Desmond's features before but as they were sitting there, it was only now that she saw a sadness in his eyes. This was hidden most of the time with the constant grin on his face, which portrayed a look of happiness. He had a deepness about him that was hard to explain. Perhaps it was because he had lost his wife, the mother of his child. They were both dreamers together and neither was stuck for words, so their friendship was getting stronger. He had a warmth about him that made Emmeline feel really comfortable around him. Little John was told to sit still a dozen times as he was so excited he kept trying to stand in the boat.

When they were halfway to the island, Desmond asked her if she would like to have a go at rowing. Emmeline had never held an oar in her hand before, so of course she didn't know where to start. Desmond sat behind her and put his arms around her and they both held the oars and after a few minutes they got a rhythm going; it was a bit awkward at the start but it didn't take her long to pick it up. She only managed to row a short distance before she handed it back to Desmond as her arms were tired. "Isn't this fun, Miss Emmeline? Daddy is a hero, isn't he? He knows everything and he is very strong." They both laughed at the little boy's remarks. "Yes, your daddy is a hero and when we get to the island he will be the king," she remarked. "Will you be his queen?" he asked. This left Emmeline in limbo. How was she going to answer this? "Look, we are nearly there," said Desmond as he pointed to the little bay where they were going to pull into the shore. That saved the day, she thought. He manoeuvred the boat near the shore and jumped into the water and pulled the boat up on the bank where he tied it to a tree. They were able to step off onto dry land. Little John jumped off first and ran around like a hen with his head chopped off, meanwhile Desmond helped Emmeline ashore.

She stood and closed her eyes and breathed the air of this beautiful island and all her feelings that had been stored for many years came flooding back. The thoughts of her mama, which she had nearly lost, came alive and she was here telling her about Isabella's wonderful life. Suddenly, she found herself running between the trees with her arms out as if she were dancing; this was her dream come true. Desmond and little John watched as she moved among the trees with her arms outstretched like a baby bird trying to fly. It was too much for Desmond so he went over and took her in his arms and they danced through the long grass twirling and dancing like two possessed souls until they fell exhausted on the grass. Little John yelled in delight and came over and plonked down in the middle of them.

The three of them lay there looking up at blue sky trying to make forms from the odd cloud that was passing by, each holding on to their own secret dreams, not wanting to share, so silence prevailed. Emmeline was dreaming of Isabella: was she up there in that vast universe, was her spirit here on the island today? she wondered. But Desmond's were quite different. He had not been this happy for a long time ... had he met his second love?

"When are we going to eat? I'm hungry!" piped up a little voice. This was the end of the dreaming. With this, Desmond jumped up and went to fetch the basket, which had been left abandoned back at the boat. He brought it over and Emmeline spread the rug on the grass and opened the lid and took out the food. They ate some of the potted meat and broke off chunks of the crusty bread and hungrily devoured it. There was no time for talk; all efforts went into filling empty stomachs. They decided to leave the cake for later. There didn't seem to be any other people on the island that they could see, but then it was a mile long.

Now it was time to explore. First, they made their way through the long grass and on to a pathway that led to the mansion. As they approached, there before them stood an unusual circular building. It was constructed of stone and was three storeys high with many lattice windows on each storey. It was a domed Georgian-styled mansion. At the entrance there was a porch-covered walkway and supporting the roof was four round columns.

"Look here, Miss Emmeline, look at those two ladies," said the excited little boy. In a niche on either side of the portico were two exquisite marble statues. "These statues represent summer and autumn. I read about these and how they bring peace and serenity to the isle," said Emmeline. They walked around to the first window and peeped in. They were looking into the huge drawing room that had a lovely ornate fireplace. The walls were panelled timber and the ceiling rose was beautiful, very decorative. There was minimal furniture in the home but there were still paintings hanging on the walls. In the next window they saw a circular archway supported by ornate carved columns and a circular wooden staircase with wrought iron rails leading up to the next floors. The floors were timber and had beautiful carpet runners which gave the mansion a stately presence. It didn't look like it was used very often, as the grounds were quite overgrown.

Little John wanted to explore the walking path that skirted the island so they left the mansion and headed down through the pink and crimson rhododendrons. Emmeline stood still for a moment surrounded by the beautiful colours, and she could feel the spirit of Isabella brooding for her beloved isle. She loved this feeling as it made her body tingle. She then ran and caught up with Desmond and little John. They walked quite a distance until a little voice said he wanted to rest, so they sat down among the long grass. As they were resting, suddenly

Emmeline remembered some of the history of the island that had come back to her, something her papa had told her.

"When they were digging the foundations for the mansion they found many bricks and some old armour which was thought to be of Roman origin. There is meant to be a Roman well in the basement. Apparently, this island and surrounding areas were occupied by the Romans many years ago," she told them. "You have so much history on the isle, I will get you to come and give a talk at the school one day. The kids should grow up with this knowledge, it should not be lost," said Desmond. "I'm tired, let's go back," said a little voice.

Little did they realise the time, or more importantly the breeze that had got up. When they saw the lake again it was choppy and there were white tops. Desmond made the decision that they would have to stay until the water calmed down, as it was too dangerous for them to attempt to cross while it was so rough. "The lake is angry now, Miss Emmeline," said little John. Desmond picked up the picnic basket and they headed back to the mansion to shelter in the front entrance. He was so annoyed that he hadn't kept his eye on the weather, but they were having such a good time. He felt irresponsible. Emmeline spread the picnic rug on the tiled patio and little John cuddled up to her and dropped off to sleep. Desmond kept apologising. "Don't worry, we are safe, that's all that matters. We will just have to wait and see what happens," she said.

They sat together and talked about the isle. As they looked into the distance, Emmeline remembered another story, so away she went ... "See all those trees planted on the Heights of Claife opposite the isle? John Christian Curwen planted forests of larches much to the annoyance of Wordsworth, who did not consider them suitable for lakeland scenery. This caused a storm of criticism from the local people, who had considered that the natural beauty of the isle had been spoilt. So, there was controversy as well as praise for his work."

The night air was starting to settle across the lake and a light fog was blowing in with the prevailing wind. Little John woke and said he was hungry, so they opened the basket and shared what was left over from lunch. They still had the cake so Emmeline cut it into pieces and hunger took over. Desmond went down to the lake but it was still too rough to row across. It was getting cooler and shivers overtook Emmeline so Desmond took his jacket off and put it around her shoulders. Little John wrapped himself in the picnic rug so he was snug. As they huddled together they were disturbed by the hoot of an owl that was residing nearby. "I'm sorry I got us into this mess," apologised a disappointed Desmond. "Don't worry, it is just a little hiccup," Emmeline assured him.

Meanwhile back home Jane was worried as it was dark and Emmeline had not returned. She could see white tops on the lake. It would be dangerous to row against those waves; she hoped Miss Emmeline was safe. As time went on she decided to walk to Mr Stenhouse's and state her concern. She knocked on his door and when he saw Jane standing there, he knew something was wrong. "I'm sorry to disturb you, Mr Stenhouse, but Miss Emmeline has not returned from a picnic on Belle Isle. I'm so worried for her. The lake has white tops, it's not safe to cross," she stated. Mr Stenhouse turned white. "Who did she go to the island with?" he asked. "She was meeting Mr Desmond and his little boy and they were rowing across to have a picnic on the island," she said. "Surely Desmond would have seen the waves coming and made it back before it got too rough. This is very irresponsible of him. I will arrange a search party and we will go down to the lake." He was worried for Miss Emmeline; he didn't want anything to happen to her, and panic set in.

Back on the island the marooned three were all huddled together under the porch of the mansion. Desmond put his arms around Emmeline to keep her warm and little John was somewhere there in the middle. To him this was an adventure and he was excited. Neither Emmeline nor Desmond was worried, as they could see the wind was dying down. They could see the lights of Bowness so knew what direction to row in. Every now and again the hoot of on owl stirred the peace, and the rustling of leaves was getting less, indicating that the wind was blowing itself out.

Desmond released his arms from around Emmeline and made his way down to the lake's edge. The water had calmed down enough for him to feel it was now safe to row back across the lake. He called for Emmeline and little John to bring everything down while he untied the boat. They climbed in and Emmeline sat up the front and little John at the back. He was so excited about coming home in the dark; he could tell his friends about this tomorrow at school. Desmond rowed as fast as he could, as he realised that people would be worried. "I really enjoyed today, it was all I dreamed of. It stirred up a feeling I have never felt before. I feel a closer connection to Isabella and her beloved isle," said a happy Emmeline.

As they got closer to Bowness they could see flames all along the beach and realised that the village people were waiting to guide the weary travellers home safely. There were cheers as they got closer and the first person

Emmeline saw was Mr Stenhouse. "Wait for an ear-bashing, he won't be able to help himself," she told Desmond with a naughty laugh. When Desmond jumped out of the boat to pull it up on the bank, Mr Stenhouse had waded out to the boat. "That was irresponsible of you, Desmond, to put Miss Emmeline's life in danger. I would have thought you would have had a greater awareness of the lake," he scolded him. Emmeline said: "There has been no harm done, we are home safe, and we all had a lovely day, it's just that we lost track of time. Thank you all for coming down, you may go home now."

Desmond lifted little John out, then came back to help Emmeline onto the bank. Mr Stenhouse took her arm and helped her up the bank. "Thank goodness you are safe, I was so worried," he whispered to her. Little John came over and took her hand and said he had a lovely day, and she bent down and gave him a cuddle and told him he was a brave boy. Desmond came over and thanked her with a hug, endorsing his son's feelings. He asked if he could take her home, but Mr Stenhouse stepped in and said he was accompanying her home. As they said their goodbyes, Mr Stenhouse stood and watched the gestures of affection given to Desmond and his son. He felt despondent that none had been bestowed on him. What did he have to do to win her affection? He asked her, "What did you do on the island all day?" "We danced among the trees until we collapsed exhausted on the grass, we walked the paths into the woods, and we lay on our backs looking up at the sky making forms out of the clouds." He didn't want to hear any more, he had heard enough. Fancy them being so irresponsible; why would anyone act in such a childish manner? He felt sick inside thinking of his cousin lying next to Miss Emmeline on the grass. It should be him lying beside her, but not on the grass.

10

Emmeline's Seventeenth Birthday

Today was Emmeline's seventeenth birthday, and only Jane and Ewan knew. He had asked to take her out for supper. This was his last night on nightshift as a collier; the following day he would start his new job as an office charge hand. This was going to be a new experience; he would miss not working with the miners down in the shafts, but to be away from the coal dust was a welcoming thought. Any complaints were for him to sort out. The nine new miners had started at Emmeline's collieries and were grateful at being employed again, although two of the younger men were quite outspoken, which was unusual for a miner, as most were humble men. Ewan would keep his eye on these men as he sensed trouble. Tonight, he was going to be down in the shafts with them to show them the ropes, so he would be wide awake to any deviations from the strict rules that applied while the men were working underground. Emmeline had told him that the uncles were still hoping to get their hands on her collieries. Was this one way they could manipulate their way towards that goal, by stirring up unrest among her miners? More than that, he didn't want any mishaps in the shafts, because this was the place where things could go horribly wrong.

Emmeline had brought a lovely new dress for tonight. She took out her braids and washed her hair and brushed it dry until it fell softly around her neck and down her back. She had family heirlooms from her mother, beautiful jewelled hairpins that she had never worn before. She had saved these for a special occasion. On her seventeenth birthday she felt this was special enough, so placed them on the side of her head, which gave her a cultured look. She was excited as well as nervous as this was her first date ... of sorts.

She sat in her favourite chair talking away to Isabella, asking her if she felt this excited on her first date. Then her mind went back to what Jane had said. It wouldn't be the first or last time she would fall in love, as this may happen more than once. She hoped she was wrong. Her friendship with Desmond was different; she enjoyed his company but he was her friend, not a lover, although she remembered the three of them huddled together on Belle Isle and how his arms had kept her warm and she felt safe. And that he had taken her in his arms and they had danced among the trees like free spirits. She couldn't imagine Ewan doing anything like that.

Jane came and announced she had a visitor. She asked

her to show him through. When he walked into the room, she wanted to throw herself into his arms; those smiling eyes said it all and his physique brought on a sense of wanting him. He was just as taken with her; she looked beautiful tonight. She had changed from a girl to a young woman. Her dress showed off her rounded breasts, something he had not noticed before, but he was drawn to, and her locks of hair fell softly around her neck. She stirred feelings within him and he knew at that moment she was definitely special. He had felt a connection at their first encounter.

"You look lovely, Miss Emmeline, happy seventeenth birthday," and he came over and gave her a kiss on her cheek. She felt colour flushing her cheeks and a weakness in her knees; this is what she had dreamed what love would be like. "Please call me Emmeline," was all she could think of to say at that moment. "Thank you, I will call you Emmeline when we are together but in the coal-pit I will call you Miss Emmeline. Come take my arm and we will go to supper," he said.

Jane watched them leave the home arm in arm. She did think Miss Emmeline looked so grown up tonight. She could see her blossoming into a lovely young lady, like her mother. Jane had just taken over this position from her mother as housemaid to the Christian household when Emmeline was a baby. Emmeline's mother was a beautiful young lady when she met Mr Christian. He was an older gentleman but he loved her dearly, and never got over losing her. He mourned for many years and never remarried. The only other lady he had was before Emmeline's mother, but she had left town. She had often wondered if the lady that came to visit him with the young lad was that lady, and that the lad was, in fact, Emmeline's half-brother. Perhaps he was the Thomas that Emmeline had mentioned. Jane had never mentioned this to anyone as she was so grateful to have such good employment. Being a Quaker did not open many doors so she gave her best to this household.

As they made their way down the road arm in arm, silence fell on them both. Ewan broke the silence and asked, "I heard at the coal-pit that you nearly didn't make it home from Belle Isle on Sunday night; what happened?" "We went to the island for the day to picnic and explore the walkways and the mansion; we got caught up in the magic of the isle and lost track of time. When it was time to row back, the lake was too choppy so we waited for the wind to abate. By this time darkness had set in, but all ended well. We had a lovely day and little John was so excited, it was a big adventure for him." "But Emmeline, what if something had happened to you? Who would look after your collieries and the miners? The lake has no friends; it draws people in then doesn't care what happens once it has them, please always remember that!" he said with passion in his voice.

Emmeline asked Ewan where they were going. "First, we are going to walk down by the lake, the rest is a surprise." As they were walking along, her heart was racing. She loved being this close to Ewan, and with her arm linked in his, she was in heaven. The evening breeze had stirred up the lake and white tops were forming. "Look at that, the lake has changed its mood in a matter of minutes, that is what I was telling you about," he warned. "It was the first time I had a chance to visit my favourite place, as I had no one to go with, so when Desmond asked me, it was a dream come true," replied Emmeline. "Is Desmond your boyfriend?" asked Ewan. "No, we are just very good friends we share similar interests; we are dreamers together," she explained. This now revealed that she was indeed a young lady who was available. Ewan had had feelings for her from the first minute he saw her at her father's burial, then when she shook his hand that day as he surfaced in the cage at the coal-pit, he felt an instant attraction. He did not know of her wealth when he first saw her, he had no idea who she was. It was not until a miner told him she was Mr Christian's daughter.

As they were walking along the shore, Emmeline remembered this area; she had been here before. Then it all came back; this was where Mr Stenhouse had dropped Ewan off after the colliery disaster. "Welcome to my home. Emmeline," he said as he opened the door. The first thing she noticed was a birthday cake sitting on the table among other goodies. Then she looked around and saw home-made banners hanging on the walls with little drawings. "Oh Ewan, this is such a lovely surprise, you have been busy, I love all this." She could not believe that a young man would go to all this trouble to make her happy. She couldn't restrain herself any longer and went to him and kissed him on the cheek. He took her in his arms and held her close, both feeling the attraction to each other. Then when she realised what she had done she withdrew and apologised for her forward behaviour. "Don't, Miss Emmeline; when two people are attracted to each other it is natural for them to show their feelings. I knew how I felt about you, I didn't know how you felt, but now I do and I'm really happy," he answered, and his smiling eyes said it all. She nestled back into him and he took her in his arms and held her close. They stood together, neither wanting to break the silence of the moment ... this wonderful moment where it all began!

"Come, Emmeline let us eat." He had baked a brown trout that he had caught in the lake earlier and as he lifted it out of the pan and laid it on the table, it smelt delicious. He broke off pieces of his home-made bread and they ate it with the trout. Emmeline loved the fresh fish. He had baked scones and made some blueberry jam to have with them. "Did you do all this yourself?" she asked. He said his mother had brought him up to fend for himself, so yes, he knew how to survive. He apologised for not baking the cake, but he had given a miner's wife some money to make it for him. "This is the best birthday ever, you have made me feel so grown up tonight, Ewan," then she started laughing as she read what was written on the banners and the little drawings done in flaky coal. "I like drawing, it makes me happy. I started when I was young and have never stopped; that is how I relax," he said. "Come, you must cut the cake, it is your birthday duty, then we can eat it." He gave Emmeline the knife and held on to her hand and they cut the cake together. He put a piece each on a plate and took it over to the settee and asked her to come and sit by him.

While they were eating Emmeline asked, "Why are you so interested in the collieries and the miners?" "I heard of so many colliery disasters I wanted to find out why men perished and how I could stop this from happening. Two of my school friends lost their fathers and I saw the hardships that befell the families, so I decided to try to make a difference so that other families didn't suffer the same peril. I wanted to work down in the shafts with the men and see first-hand how dangerous it was. I now know that a lot of these disasters need not have happened if proper safety procedures were in place. The reason why I have stayed so long at your collieries is because I want to point out in my thesis that bosses have to change and put the men's safety before their profits. It can be done, your collieries are the best example, and if the miners are treated with respect then that respect comes back to the bosses," he said with passion. "We need the government to pass a bill that will make all collieries as safe as they can be, and that safety inspectors visit each colliery and close them down if they don't comply with the safety standards set by the ruling bodies. This is what I am pushing for; there must be more rights for the men who risk their lives to go underground. They are humans, not packhorses, and must be treated as such. If the workers don't stand up for their rights, nothing happens. It was only three years ago when legislation was passed to ban children under the age of ten from working in the collieries, and to think half of them weren't even paid, it breaks my heart that such practices even existed. But there are some pretty ruthless bosses out there, and we must stop them from exploitation of the miners. I want to make a difference to these men's lives, Emmeline, this cannot go on as it is."

She stood in awe of this man's passion to stand up for the rights of the miners. Papa would have loved him as I do, she thought to herself. "It is so good to meet a man so passionate about the miners and their wellbeing; you have won my heart, Ewan," she told him with the upmost truth. He came over and took her hand and they both sat on the settee and cuddled up together. She didn't ever want to leave this little cottage by the lake, but most of all she didn't want to leave Ewan. Time was creeping on so they had to make a move, as he had to start work at midnight. She stood on her tiptoes and kissed him on the lips. His response was what she wanted to happen: he pulled her close and kissed her passionately. She was overcome with happiness. He had to stop himself before he became too deeply involved.

"Come, my dear Emmeline, we must go or I will be late for work, my boss might sack me." On his saying this, they both laughed. They walked to her home hand in hand, both happy to share their closeness. On reaching Emmeline's home they kissed each other and said their farewells. Emmeline had never been so happy; now she knew what love felt like.

Jane was waiting to see that she arrived home safely before she went to bed. "Jane, I had the most wonderful birthday. Ewan cooked me tea, we ate a trout he had caught in the lake, and ate scones he had baked, then we talked until it was time to leave. He has made me so happy. I am in love with him and I know he likes me back. We held each other close and we kissed. You know, Jane, he is a very caring young man; he wants to change the working conditions for the miners, so he is going to present his case to Parliament for new law changes. He is all for the miners and their plight," said an excited Emmeline. Jane listened and thought that he seemed a sensible young man, and hoped Miss Emmeline wasn't reading too much into his feelings for her. The fact that she loved him didn't secure his love for her ... was she being too eager? Emmeline was a lovely young lady who would attract much attention, but her wealth would bring suitors whose love for money would exceed their love for her. This was just the start ... where would it end? Before Emmeline went to bed, she made her way to the drawing room to talk about her night to Isabella. Now she knew what it felt like to be in love; this was another secret they shared. Their lives were still similar, although Emmeline had fallen in love with a total stranger, not a cousin like Isabella had.

That night at the collieries, all did not go as well as Ewan would have liked. One of the new men thought he knew more than Ewan and did not do what was asked of him. No one had ever argued with him as he knew the safety procedures; they were put there to protect the miners. Because this new arrival had worked in Emmeline's uncles' colliery, where safety was not a priority, and he had more years as a miner than Ewan, he would not take orders. The misunderstanding started when Ewan showed him the barometer that changed if gas levels rose, as this was an indication that there was a build-up of methane. It was a valuable safety precaution that had to be checked every hour, and this was part of his job description. He told Ewan he thought it was a bit over the top to have to come back here and check it so often, as it had to be recorded every time it was checked. He let the miner know that all safety precautions had to be followed by the rule book. This was how things worked in this colliery. Unfortunately, this was Ewan's last night underground and this worried him; was this one of the narks he had heard about?

As Emmeline stirred, the sun had already risen and was shining in her bedroom. She lay there thinking about last night. Gosh, Ewan was passionate about the safety of the miners, and this prompted her to go to visit some of the widows from her uncles' colliery disaster, as she had promised. His talk had spurred her on to help those families that were suffering. He had experienced the hardships that had befallen families, like his school friends who had lost their fathers. She climbed out of bed and sat and braided her hair, then put on a plain dress. She went to the stables and asked the groundsman to get the carriage ready, that they were going on a mission. On the way they called at the colliery store and purchased some food vouchers that she asked to be charged to her account. She would give these to families in need.

As they proceeded along the rough gravel roads to where a lot of the miners lived, she could not believe the poverty in this area. There were no gardens, just long grass and overgrown pathways. The first home they stopped at, little kids were fighting in the back yard. Their mother was yelling at them and when she saw Emmeline she apologised. She told Emmeline the kids were hungry as they had very little food now that they had no one to provide for them. This broke her heart to hear this, so she gave them vouchers to get food from the colliery store. Each home she called at she heard the same story; no one cared about the families who had lost their breadwinners ... they were the forgotten!

She decided with all her wealth she would help these families make a better life. If she could set up a little farmlet where the children could care for the animals, that would ultimately provide food for their tables. The women could grow vegetables and flowers, which would make their lives worthwhile. A little colour in the garden would shed a ray of hope. Emmeline knew the joy she received as she walked in her garden among the roses and bedding plants. She decided to have an open day at her home and asked her groundsman to show the women how they could achieve the same results, but on a smaller scale. She would provide each family with a rose bush and some vegetable plants and flower seeds. She would pay six unemployed men to put up fences and she would supply the wire, posts and the timber for them to build hen houses and pig pens. Then she would go to the Ambleside markets on Saturday and buy some stock. Emmeline would ask Desmond and little John to accompany her, as Desmond would know more about livestock than she did. Perhaps they could even buy a couple of cows, then they could have milk for the children. These poor people had no money to buy anything other than what they could afford, which wasn't even enough to feed them, so unless someone helped, they went without. She would not ask Mr Stenhouse; all he had to do was pay the accounts when they came in. She knew his stance on the working class. When it was time to ask questions, it would all be too late, there would be no going back.

Emmeline had not caught up with Desmond since their boating adventure to Belle Isle. She had not been down to the lake to her favourite spot, as other things had taken up her time, but today she made her way down hoping to catch up with him and little John. It wasn't long before she heard her name being called. "Miss Emmeline, I told my friends about our adventure and rowing back in the dark. They thought it would have been scary," he yelled full of enthusiasm. "I've missed you, little John. Yes, we had a lovely day, didn't we? Where is your father?" she asked. "He told me to come and see if you were here. He fell and hurt his ankle so he can't walk for a couple of days," he said in a sad voice. "Can I come back with you to see him?" she asked. "Yes, he would like that. Come with me," he replied.

He took her hand and led her back along the lake, through a large park to a quaint little area, to 13 Witford Street. He opened the door and called, "Daddy, you have a visitor, someone special." This made Emmeline laugh, what a dear little boy. There was Desmond sitting in a chair with his leg up on a stool. "What happened to you?" she asked. "I tripped over someone's bag at school; they had left it on the floor. I just have to rest for a couple of days, then I should be fine," he said. "How are you, Emmeline, did you get scolded by cousin Edward?" he asked. "Yes, he gave me a stern talking to, he told me I should be more of a lady than what I am." This brought on laughter from them both. She asked if she could help in any way, but he told her everything was under control. Emmeline asked if they were free the following weekend and if they'd like to come to Ambleside to the markets to buy some livestock for the farmlet she was setting up for the families without breadwinners. This would occupy the children and give them some sense of hope for the future.

"That sounds wonderful, Emmeline, we would love to come. You are so kind to share what you have with the poorer village people. I see it at school, some of the children only make it for one day out of the week because they can't afford any more. All children should be able to attend school. Without schooling, their futures look bleak; they will end up in collieries just like their fathers. They at least deserve a choice," he said in earnest. "I was lucky my mother's family had money and they were able to support her, as her husband — my father — died when I was a baby. No one talked about him, it was a closed book, so I didn't ask any questions. But I did have a choice and for that I am truly grateful." "That's what I like about you, Desmond, you feel for others and you are a good father to your son." "I love my little boy, sometimes he is the only thing that keeps my head above water. After I lost my wife my world came crashing down, but I had to stay strong for him," he said in a quiet voice. This was the sadness she had noticed in his eyes. "One day you will meet someone else who will love you and little John for the good people that you are," she said with a tear in her eye. If she hadn't met

Ewan she felt she could have loved Desmond. They got on really well together and had so many things in common. Desmond's thoughts were in a way similar to hers, as he knew he had found his next love ... but did she know? Of course, he didn't know she had fallen in love with Ewan. It was time for Emmeline to leave for home so she bent down and gave him a hug and said she would see them the following weekend when they went to the markets. As she was leaving she noticed two family photos with a couple and a little baby, and tears formed in her eyes.

Several days had passed and the fences were going along nicely, the men were happy to be making a little money. Emmeline's papa had bought all the land surrounding the miners' cottages so the land was there to be used. The next project was the building of the pig pens and hen houses. This would take less than a week to construct, and there was much excitement within the neighbouring properties. A meeting would be held to work out a roster for each household to take turns at caring for the animals.

Meanwhile, Mr Stenhouse had received an account for many food vouchers that had been cashed at the colliery store and charged to Miss Emmeline. He would call at her home after work and see what this was all about. What was she up to now? As he made his was to her home he was looking forward to seeing her, as it had been nearly two weeks since their last meeting. He knocked on the door and Jane opened it. "Is Miss Emmeline in?" he asked politely. "I'm sorry, Mr Stenhouse, she said she was going to visit Mr Desmond as she had something to discuss with him." What would she want to discuss with his cousin? he wondered. Surely, she would come to him first, he was her business adviser; what would Desmond know? With this he tipped his hat to Jane and thanked her. "Would you ask her to come to my office tomorrow morning, please?" She agreed to pass the message on to Miss Emmeline.

The next morning before going to the coal-pit, Emmeline stopped off at Mr Stenhouse's office as requested. She knew what it would be about so she had prepared herself. He asked her into his office and closed the door. "Miss Emmeline, I have an account here from the colliery store for many food vouchers. Can you explain why you have to pay them?" he asked. "Certainly. I went to visit the widows that were left after my uncles' colliery disaster and they were living in such poverty, the children were starving, so I decided to issue some food vouchers so the children could be fed. I will not stand by and see children starving," she stated. "But Miss Emmeline, you cannot feed everyone, there will always be hungry families," he answered. "Mr Stenhouse, just to let you know, there will more amounts for netting, posts and building materials, as well as livestock."

She told him what she was doing for the families to give them a chance to grow their own vegetables, and get eggs and milk from the animals, as well as meat. He sat there stunned. Since when had she taken on the worries of the miners' families? "Miss Emmeline, as kind as this may seem, it all costs money," he told her. "Yes, I know and it is my money I am spending. Desmond and little John are coming to the markets next Saturday and we are going to buy the livestock. The paddocks are all ready as are the buildings to house the animals," she said with pride. When did she arrange all this? Why hadn't he been told? He was quite hurt about the whole thing. "Did you not feel you could talk about this with me?" he asked her. Emmeline told him it was something she wanted to do on her own now that she was seventeen. "Oh, Emmeline, why didn't you tell me? I would have asked you out to celebrate!" he said. "Thank you, Mr Stenhouse, but Ewan cooked me supper. We had a lovely night at his cottage." Just the mention of Ewan brought on a bad belt of twitches. She could see by his face he was not happy. "Please pay the account to the colliery store and we will discuss the rest when they come in. I'm on my way to the coal-pit now," and she bid him farewell.

He was broken-hearted; he wanted to shed his hidden tears right there in his office, but it would not be proper. He was so jealous of Ewan, he hated even hearing his name. How could he win Miss Emmeline's heart? Perhaps he could arrange to take her out to a posh eating house where they could be seen as society socialites. He would be so happy to have her on his arm, and to know she was probably the wealthiest of all that were there. He would ask her next time she called at his office, then he would make arrangements with some of his upper-class friends to join them for a pre-dinner drink.

Emmeline couldn't wait to get to the coal-pit office to see Ewan. She was surprised to learn that he had gone down the shafts at the change of shifts. Why would he do that? she wondered. That meant she wouldn't see him today. She felt disappointed. She went home and sat at her papa's desk and worked out how much it would cost to send twelve children to school for a year. It would be an opportunity that these children would not otherwise have. If it was successful she would then help more children with an opportunity to be educated. She knew this would make a huge difference to some of the underprivileged village children. Emmeline would give first preference to the children who had no fathers, as they were the ones missing out on so much. She felt perhaps she should talk to Mr Stenhouse, as he seemed upset that she hadn't included him in her farmlet project.

The next morning she called at his office and was asked to come through. "How are you this morning, Miss Emmeline?" he asked. Nothing was going to upset him today; he had a plan in place that involved her. "I'm fine thank you. I wanted to discuss with you what I am planning. I want to pay for twelve of the village children to attend school for a year as a trial. If it is successful then I will help more the following year," she said. "But Miss Emmeline, this will cost a lot of money," he said; he couldn't help himself. "I know how much it will cost and it will be money well spent. I have nothing else to spend my money on and I want to share it with the children. Don't you think that is a wonderful idea, Mr Stenhouse?" she asked. He didn't know what to say. Children were never in his equation, but if he was to win her heart, he would probably have to think differently, as she might want children of her own one day. He didn't want to upset her, better to agree and try to win her that way, he thought. "If that is what you want to do for the children, then do it," he said. This took her by surprise as she expected a negative answer. Was Mr Stenhouse mellowing in his middle age? she wondered. "Oh, by the way, Miss Emmeline, I would like to take you out to dinner one night next week as a belated birthday present," he suggested. "Would Thursday night suit you? I will pick you up in my carriage and we will ride into Ambleside." Before she realised, she had accepted his invitation. This will be a boring night, she told herself, but what was one night out of her life to spend with Mr Stenhouse?

Ewan had elected to go down into the shaft separate to the shift changeover as he had been told the barometer was not being checked regularly. This was a major safety precaution so had to be treated as such. He waited at the safety station to see if the miner came and checked on the hour, but two hours had passed and he had not seen him. On the third hour he arrived and got a shock to see Ewan there. "Thought you'd catch me out?" he said in a snide voice. Ewan asked him if he had checked on each hour and he assured him he had. "I have been here for three hours and this is your first visit within this time. You know the rules; if you don't abide by them there is no place in this colliery for you. Safety is paramount. You have been warned!" Ewan told him sternly. He did not like or trust this man. He stayed and worked with the miners and came up with them at midnight when the shift changed over. He hoped to see Emmeline tomorrow as he wanted her to come to his cottage.

11

Feelings are Stirring within Emmeline

It was Friday night and as arranged Emmeline had walked down to Ewan's cottage; she was so looking forward to spending time with him. He had put two chairs on the porch where they could sit and look at the lake as they talked. It was a lovely evening and the lake was behaving perfectly, there wasn't so much as a ripple; that was until a fish surfaced to catch his supper and a swirl appeared in the water. Ewan greeted her with a kiss and they sat holding hands. Emmeline kept him up to date with how the farmlet was progressing. He was proud of her for helping the families suffering hardships. Together they had the wellbeing of others at heart. It was the perfect match. "You know, Ewan, I wish Papa could have met you, he would have approved of you. He was a caring man like yourself; all he wanted was his collieries to be a place where the miners were happy to come to work. He knew how hard it was for the men to work underground all day, so their wellbeing and safety were paramount to him. That is why he didn't want his brothers running his collieries. He was the only man to supply transport to and from the coal-pit at the end of every shift, because he cared for his men. He would have loved you, as I do," she said earnestly. With this he asked her to come and share his chair, and he enclosed her in his arms. Emmeline loved being this close to Ewan; she wasn't sure what would come next, but she remembered what the girls talked about at boarding school. It was okay for him to want to touch her breasts, that was part of falling in love.

Meanwhile out of respect for Emmeline, Ewan had to hold back on his feelings, as he didn't know if she was naïve, or that because she didn't have a mother to tell her what happened when two people loved each other, she just seemed so innocent. It was no trouble to him as his feelings told him what was happening, men just seemed to know. Besides, she was only seventeen; did she fully understand the consequences of falling in love? Perhaps he would have to wait until he felt he could talk to her as to what might happen. At the moment she seemed happy just to be held in his arms and kissed passionately, but how long could he hold back for? He was a young man of twenty-five years of age and was certainly ready for a full-on relationship. Emmeline was different; she was a wealthy heiress, perhaps the richest young lady in all of Cumbria, but at heart she was just an ordinary girl who wanted ordinary things. She was not afraid to share her wealth with the village people who were suffering. He would never put his wants before his respect for her, so he was prepared to wait.

As they snuggled up in the chair together, strange things were happening in Emmeline's body. She felt aroused, she wanted Ewan to touch her bare skin, to put his hand inside her dress and touch her breasts, but he didn't. Could she take his hand and put it there, would that be wrong of her? She so wanted this to happen and her feelings were telling her to let him know what she wanted. So, she took his hand and put it inside the top of her dress, where she wanted to be touch. He responded by caressing her and she knew then, that's what she wanted, to feel his hands on her bare skin, for him to be touching a secret part of her body. Ewan was taken by surprise, he had not seen this coming. Perhaps she was ready to move on in their relationship, but he would let her tell him when she was ready for whatever came next.

It was time to move inside and not be on display in public. This was something beautiful that was happening between the two of them. "I wanted you to touch me, Ewan, my body told me so, please don't think bad of me," she said tenderly. "Emmeline, this is what happens between two people who love each other; feelings take over and their bodies know when it is time for things to happen. But both parties must agree. I am worried because I don't know how much you know without having had a mother to explain things to you," he said. "Don't be afraid, Ewan, I have read romantic books and I found a medical journal in Papa's drawer, which I read. It was quite sad reading things from a book, but I didn't have anyone to talk to me. Papa would probably have told me if he was still here, but then I don't know. It's probably a mother thing," she said in a sad voice. "I will never take anything from you that you don't want to give; I respect you, Emmeline. That we can talk about these things makes our bond even stronger," he said sincerely. They sat together both enjoying this 'touching' moment. Emmeline felt good about herself, it just seemed so natural; she wasn't afraid or ashamed. Soon it was time for Ewan to walk her home.

Today was market day. Desmond and little John had arrived and they were down at the stables getting the horses and cart ready. Emmeline's groundsman had told them to take the cart if they were bringing livestock back, but he said he didn't know where the cows were going to fit. They all laughed at this remark. Desmond was in charge; the cows would be tied behind the cart and they would walk them home. It was going to be a big day but they were ready for it. Away they went, the three of them sitting together on the front seat of the cart. Emmeline was sitting next to Desmond and little John sat on the outside. "This is like riding with my daddy and mummy," he said. Desmond snuck a quick look at Emmeline to see the reaction on her face and he was pleased to see her smiling. "Yes, it's like we are a family going to the market," she answered. Little John started singing some school songs and they all sang along, some in tune, some not, but to see the happiness on this little boy's face was rewarding enough.

Emmeline had a list of things she had to get: vegetable plants, flower seeds, rose bushes, wheat and the livestock. They pulled up at the place where all the horses and carts were tied up and let the horses drink from the water trough, before feeding them hay. They then walked to the markets. Little John made straight to the pens with the livestock. He squealed with delight at the pen full of piglets. But suddenly Emmeline had to think hard on this: there would not be enough leftovers from the households to feed four pigs, as there was barely enough food for the people themselves. She asked Desmond what he thought. "Yes, Emmeline, that is a problem; perhaps if we get two piglets as company for one another. We will ask the businesses if we could get their scraps," he suggested. They both decided they would be better to buy some sheep as all they ate was grass, and there was plenty of that. They let little John pick out two piglets and put them in a box. Then they made their way over to the poultry. They chose twelve hens and put six in each wire cage. The man selling the sheep offered to deliver the eight sheep on Tuesday as he had a pen on his cart, so that solved that problem. Now for the cows. They didn't have much knowledge on what to buy, so Desmond asked the man to milk a couple of cows so he could see they had milk. He laughed at Desmond and explained that the cows were in calf so they were making milk. This meant they would get a couple of calves in a few months' time. They settled for two and as Desmond and his son walked the cows to the cart and tied them up, Emmeline went and bought the vegie plants and seeds. The horticulture man was coming to Bowness next week so he would deliver the rose bushes to her home. Now for the wheat. She bought two bags and asked the young man if he would carry them to her cart. She was a pretty young thing so he agreed, but he was disappointed when he carried the bags over only to find she had a husband and a young son!

Emmeline had passed a stall selling sweeties so bought little John a treat. She would give them to him on the way home as it was going to be a slow trip. After they finished at the markets they started on their homeward journey. Little John sat at the back of the cart and told the cows they were too slow. The piglets were squealing in the box and the hens were trying to flutter around in their cages sending feathers flying everywhere. It was like Old McDonald's farm. At the halfway point it was too much for little John so he came up to the front seat and cuddled into Emmeline. She gave him the sweeties she had bought and he sucked them as he cuddled closer. Desmond looked across at him and it brought tears to his eyes; little John was missing a mother's love, and here was a lovely lady who could fill that void. Little John adored Emmeline, she was so caring towards him; he was feeling that motherly bond that was missing. As they were entering Bowness he asked, "Miss Emmeline, do you have a boyfriend?" She didn't know what to say, but felt it was best to tell the truth. "Yes, Mr Fletcher is my boyfriend." "I wish Daddy was your boyfriend, then you could be my mummy," he said in a sad voice. "It doesn't matter who my boyfriend is, I love you, little John, and your daddy; we are very good friends and always will be," she said. When Desmond heard that Emmeline and Mr Fletcher were together he had to turn away to hide his tears. He had hoped she could have been his girlfriend as she was the first person who he felt really close to since losing his wife, in fact he had fallen for her. He would live in hope that perhaps one day they could be together, but to be good friends was important for the moment.

They drove the horses through the gate and into the paddock where they untied the cows, the poor things were so weary. Desmond carried the box with the piglets over to the pig pen and let them out; they were like a couple of mad things tearing here and there squealing like mad. The hens were next. As Desmond lifted the cages up, there were a couple of eggs in the back of the cart. "Look, Miss Emmeline, the hens have left a present for us" and he went and picked them up. Standing at the fence watching all that was going on were two little boys from the miners' cottages, so little John took the eggs over and gave them one each. They ran inside calling to their mother who came out to thank him. Emmeline told her that eight sheep would be arriving on Tuesday to be put into the paddock. "The cows will be ready to milk tomorrow. I will come and see you in the morning," Emmeline told her, and the lady thanked her for her kindness.

She went over to little John and picked him up and cuddled him. "You are a very good boy for sharing the eggs with other children. Your father has brought you up well, you are a lucky boy to have such a good daddy," she said lovingly. "Yes, I love him too," he answered. As they drove out the gate, Emmeline closed it and climbed onto the cart as they made their way back to her stables. They unhitched the horses, gave them a drink and fed them some hay. Everyone had had a big day and they were all tired. She asked Desmond to come in for a cup of tea, but he said he would take little John home to bed. She came over to him and thanked him for a great day and gave him a hug. He hugged her back and didn't want to let go, then he remembered Mr Fletcher so quickly pulled away. Little John came to her to get his goodbye hug, then Desmond put him on his back and piggybacked him towards home.

Emmeline was home on Tuesday when the horticultural man came with the rose bushes. He talked to her and asked where she was going to plant them. She told him they weren't for her, they were for the widows who had lost their husbands in the colliery disaster. She thought they might bring a ray of sunshine to their lives, along with the vegetable plants and flower seeds. "You are a kind person to care for the widows; not many of the middle class or upper class cast a thought their way, they are the forgotten," he said. Emmeline noted that he was a well-spoken man, probably middle class and about thirty years of age. "Do you know where Mr Edward Stenhouse's office is?" he asked. "Oh, you know him?" she asked. "Yes, we went to school together, we often meet in town at business meetings. He is a very clever man, not at all light-hearted, in fact a little dull. He needs to meet a young lady, in fact he is bringing an influential young lady to dinner on Thursday night. We are all going to meet for drinks, we can't wait to see who is on his arm," he said with a laugh. "By the way, I am George." Emmeline told him the way to Mr Stenhouse's office, not wanting to volunteer her name. Fancy Mr Stenhouse and this man attending school together. Mr Stenhouse looked much older; perhaps he wasn't that old after all. This made her think about her Thursday night date. She always had thoughts about shocking him to see if he had any emotions at all in his upper-class body. She would work on this!

12

Mr Stenhouse

Thursday night had arrived and Emmeline had talked herself into behaving in an upper-class manner while mixing with elite. She had bought a beautiful new dress with a tight-fitting bodice that showed off her firm breasts. This would be a talking point; she would do Mr Stenhouse justice tonight. She let her hair fall in soft ringlets around her neck and shoulders; she looked like a painting. When Jane came to announce Mr Stenhouse had arrived, she asked Jane to ask him in. As he walked into the drawing room he could not believe his eyes. Before him stood the vision of absolute beauty; he was stunned. "Good evening, Mr Stenhouse," she said full of confidence. He just stood and nothing would come from his mouth, and he was conscious of what was going to happen next. He had to look away until his twitches subsided. "You look lovely tonight, Miss Emmeline," he managed to say. Then when he settled down he asked her, "Miss Emmeline, do you think we could drop the formalities for one night? I would like you to call me Edward." "That is fine, and you may call me Emmeline," she said. "Come, we must be on our way," he reminded her. They walked out to the carriage and he helped her climb up; while doing this his hand brushed her bottom and he apologised profusely for his inappropriate behaviour. "Don't be so fussy, Edward, we are both adults. These things happen."

They rode in silence for a while until Emmeline asked him how he became her papa's solicitor. He told her his father had been Mr Christian's solicitor for many years and when he passed away, Mr Christian asked that the business stay on at their office and for him to take over. There was a plan in place between the two old gentlemen; they both hoped that Edward would take Emmeline to be his wife. Edward knew of Mr Christian's wishes, but she was only a child. That was until she took over the collieries, and then she suddenly grew up. But today she had blossomed into this lovely young woman with all the appropriate pieces in the right places. He felt so proud of her and now he knew why he couldn't wait for her to come to his office. How long could he hide his feelings for her? Could he compete with Mr Fletcher and his cousin Desmond? They were both outgoing young men and he had seen Emmeline embrace them both. She had never bestowed any of her affections on him and he felt this deeply. Why was it so hard for him to unleash how he felt? Perhaps because he had never seen it at home. His father was a solicitor of upper-class standing and his mother was the dutiful wife that did as she was told. He ruled with an iron hand and Edward sometimes thought his mother was afraid of him, as he was, most of the time. His voice was gruff and everything he barked out was cut short as if he didn't want to waste his final words on anyone. This left those close to him unsure of themselves. He even told Edward he had to become a solicitor so that he would follow in his footsteps, so he had no say on his chosen career. This probably explained why Edward was so stuffy, and had no confidence in himself; he had been suppressed. His mind thought a lot of things and his body told him at times that he needed to act, but putting it all together was the problem. But the biggest problem of all being his twitches. If he got upset they came on and when he was excited they started, he couldn't shake them off. Were these brought on by his uptight manner? He didn't know the answer to this … was he ever going to find out?

As they arrived at Mannerhouse Inn, Edward alighted from the carriage and tied his horses to a tethering post. This was where he had arranged to have a few drinks with his friends. He then came around and helped Emmeline down and she sensed he was uptight so leaned towards him and whispered. "Thank you, Edward, you are a true gentleman," and she gave him a friendly hug. This was more than he could have wished for; his heart started racing and funny things were happening in his body. He was in shock, he had to pull himself together. Here he was with this beautiful heiress, he should be the proudest man wanting to show her off; instead he was a quivering jellyfish. Unbeknown to Edward, Emmeline knew what was ahead of her because of her conversation with George, the horticultural man. She took Edward's arm and wrapped hers around his and led him towards the door. She was a tower of strength, while he was still quivering. "It's all right, Edward, I won't let you down," she whispered. "But I have let you down, Miss Emmeline," he stammered. "Come, Edward, we will show them," she said with confidence, and walked tall and proud into the foyer with him on her arm. This was wrong, he thought, it should have been Emmeline on his arm.

He had to excuse himself and dashed off leaving her standing alone. He ran into the men's room and gave himself a good dressing down. What had happened to him? He was behaving like a child; what a stupid man, he told himself. What did Emmeline think of him? He was so embarrassed and his twitches were going to town. He wanted to run away and hide but he couldn't leave Emmeline there on her own. He took deep breaths and tried to pull himself together. Perhaps if he got a couple of stiff whiskies in, it would help him. He recovered enough to walk back into the foyer; that was until he saw his beautiful Emmeline again. She was standing where he had left her and she smiled at him as he came over to her. "Everything is fine, Edward, just relax and enjoy yourself, I'm not going to bite you," she said in a teasing manner.

With this, some of his friends came forward, as everyone was talking about his date. Apparently, she was an influential young lady and they all wanted to meet her. They stopped in their steps when they saw Emmeline. Where did Edward get her? She was so young and pretty, not boring old Edward's type, one would have thought! He went to introduce her and stammered, so Emmeline came to his rescue. "Pleased to meet you, I'm Emmeline. Edward and I are old friends," she said. Someone slipped him a stiff whisky, which he swallowed down. They made their way over to where the rest of the party had gathered. "You old dark horse, Edward, where have you been hiding this young lady?" someone asked. "This is Miss Emmeline Christian, she is a friend of mine," he said proudly.

As soon as the name Christian was mentioned, a hush

came over the group. Everyone knew this name; it spelt money and plenty of it. Now it was time to hush the group again. She walked over to George. "Hello, George, fancy us meeting again," she said. Everyone looked at George, especially the lady accompanying him. Edward was stunned; how did George know Emmeline? This was bizarre! "George was at my home earlier this week," she announced, leaving it at that. Let these upper-class peasants draw what they liked from this. "Would you like a drink, Emmeline? What can I get you?" Edward asked. "A wine would be lovely," she answered. Everyone was chatting and she looked across at George. He stood there smiling. There had been no mention as to why they had met, or how they had met; let them have their moment of gossip, she thought. A posh lady came up to her and asked her what she did for a living. When she said she worked at the collieries, the conversation was cut short and she moved on. Thank goodness, thought Emmeline. She had not mixed with many upper-class ladies before and all they talked about was who had what, and on and on they gossiped.

She decided to add a little disruption to the evening. "Excuse me, everyone. This year I am supporting twelve children from the mining community to attend school. They have lost their fathers in colliery disasters and their mothers can't afford to school them, so I want to help give these children a chance. How do you feel about these children? Would you like to give a small donation to help their cause?" she asked. George came over and stood by Emmeline. "Emmeline bought some rose bushes off me to give to the widows for their garden to bring a little ray of sunshine to their lives. She has set up a farmlet to give them a chance to produce their own meat, milk their own cows, along with caring for hens and sheep. These families are struggling and I think we could all help out with a donation." They all clapped and put their hands in their pockets. "I would like to thank you all. I will tell the children you contributed to their cause, for this they will be very grateful," said a happy Emmeline. They came over to Edward, congratulating him on his choice of a lady friend; they thought she was a very intelligent lady. By this time, he had quite a bit of Dutch courage behind him so he went up to Emmeline and put his arm around her. She had never consumed alcohol before and now she was on her second glass. For one moment she forgot who Edward was and leaned over and placed a kiss on his cheek. To him this was the most exciting thing that had happened to him in years. As he looked down his eyes fixed on her breasts; if only they were alone, he would ask for her permission to kiss them. His mind was conjuring up naughty thoughts which he thought were not appropriate ... for goodness' sake, Edward!

Two hours had passed and Edward excused himself and Emmeline, as it was time for them to dine. As they made their way to the dining area, Edward rushed in front and lifted out her chair for her to sit down. By this time and a few whiskies later he had loosened up a bit and was coping much better. He explained the menu to her and told her to choose whatever she wanted. She noticed now that he was relaxed, his twitches were non-existent. "I am so proud of you, Emmeline, you look so lovely and grown up tonight. But tell me, how did you know George?" "I know that you and George went to school together. Are you the same age?" she quizzed. Edward wondered why she asked this; did she think he looked older than his friend? "Why do you ask?" "I'm going to be truthful, I thought you were much older than him, but as you relax I can see that you are not. That is the thing about you, Edward, you are so stuffy, so prim and proper; let your guard down and do ordinary things, things that make you happy. Are you a happy person?" As Emmeline had had two wines she was starting to babble, but she wanted to say things as she saw them. "No, I am not a happy person, I have trouble expressing my feelings and I know I am stuffy. My father was not at all like your father, I was frightened of him." Emmeline felt sad for him so reached across the table and held his hand. "I'm sorry to hear that, Edward, but don't let it spoil your life, let it all go," she told him tenderly. With this show of empathy from her, something happened within, allowing Edward to do what he wanted most: he bent down and kissed her hand. She could see this was a huge step for him. "That is so sweet, Edward." This was the first barrier broken and a little confidence emerged.

As they were eating their dinner, Emmeline couldn't take her eyes off Edward. He was dissecting his food and arranging it into little piles on his plate before he ate it. Why would he do that? she wondered. It got the better of her and she just had to ask. "Why do you play with your food before you eat it?" "What do you mean?" he asked. "Edward, you are not in your office now, you don't have to arrange your food like your papers. For goodness' sake, mess up your life a little; see, you are even stuffy at the table." Poor Edward, any steps he may have taken forward were now steps backward. He told her, "This is the way I live my life, I am a sad person, I know this. I was married once, Emmeline, but my wife left me for another man; she said I was boring." "She was right, Edward, you are boring and stuffy. For goodness' sake, do something stupid, something out of your comfort zone. Do you dance?" "I have never tried, so I don't know." "It's time you found out. When we get home, I will put some music on and we will dance," she warned him. The bubbles in the wine were dancing around in her head, giving her all the encouragement she needed to see a new Edward emerge.

They finished dining and she thanked him for an enjoyable night. As he walked over to get the carriage, she noticed he was a bit unsteady on his feet. Perhaps the whisky had clouded his mind; this might be the time to have a little fun, she thought. He brought the carriage to the front entrance, then got down to help Emmeline climb up. He pushed her up by her bottom, but there were no apologies this time; he had forgotten his manners, but this was good. When he tried to climb up on his side he was having trouble and let out a couple of swear words, then apologised profusely. "Good on you, Edward, say what you feel. If you are angry, say angry words," she encouraged him. It took several more tries before he made it. As they made their way along the road, Emmeline started singing and it wasn't long before she heard a muffled sound coming from his mouth. "Come on, Edward, be happy; belt it out." She moved closer to him and put her arm in his, and they sang like an out-of-tune choir, and he was actually laughing and enjoying himself. They carried on like this until they pulled up outside Emmeline's home. "Remember, Edward, we are going to have some dancing lessons," she reminded him.

As he dismounted from the carriage, he stumbled and fell to the ground. Emmeline jumped down and ran around to see if he was all right, but he just lay there. She tried to lift him but he wouldn't move. She ran into the home and called for Jane. She came running out and between them they half carried and half dragged Edward into a spare bedroom, and lay him on the bed. He was sound asleep. Jane stood and looked at him and started to giggle, as did Emmeline. He looked in disarray, a total different look to what they were used to. In fact, he had taken on a rugged look, one that actually suited him. Jane bent down and took off his shoes and Emmeline fetched a rug to put over him, then they left and closed the door. Outside the door they both burst into laughter. Imagine how he would feel in the morning when he found out he had stayed at her place for the night; there would not be enough words in the dictionary to cover his apologies. He would feel so ashamed of himself. Emmeline took the horses down to the stables and watered and fed them before going to bed herself.

Edward stirred in the morning with wonderful memories of his special night with Emmeline. She had even kissed him and he had kissed her hand, something he had wanted to do in his office one day when he held her soft, warm hand. Then he remembered them singing and laughing together on the way home, she had her arm around his, but what happen from then on ... he couldn't remember. He hoped he had delivered her home safely and had done nothing to shame himself. As he went to reach for his clock to see what the time was, it was not where it should have been, so he kept fidgeting around; perhaps he had knock it down last night. He opened his eyes and what a shock: where was he? This wasn't his bedroom, and when he looked down and saw he was still in his suit, he went into panic mode. Suddenly, there was a knock on the door, and as it opened he hid under the rug. Whose home was he in?

"Good morning, Edward, what a night we had, you

actually enjoyed yourself. You swore in anger and laughed in fun, that's the fun Edward I like." He could not believe what he was hearing. Was he here at Emmeline's home? Was this Emmeline in his bedroom; no, in her bedroom? "Come out from under the rug, it's no use hiding, the damage has been done." "What damage?" he asked as he emerged from under the rug. He looked so different; his hair was unruly and he looked lost. Then it all started to come back and he remembered falling from the carriage. "What can I say, I'm so embarrassed, what a stupid man I am. Emmeline, I wanted everything to be so special last night, what a mess I have made, please forgive me, I'm so sorry." "Don't be sorry, we both had a good night. You are a different person when you forget your stuffy ways; you were actually a lot of fun. I had thought it was going to be a boring night but it was far from it." She went and fetched his shoes and took them over to him. He reached for her hands. "I hope, Miss Emmeline, I didn't embarrass you too much, I can hardly look at you." "Mr Stenhouse, it was a nice night. You had fun and I had fun, let us remember it for what it was; forget the negatives, focus on the positives. Now get yourself home, it is time you were at work." She accompanied him to the stables to get his horses. Before he climbed into the carriage he came around and kissed her on the forehead. "You are the sweetest girl, Emmeline." "And you, Edward, are a good man."

13

A Sudden Call-out

Today was Friday and Emmeline had agreed to visit Ewan at his cottage. She was looking forward to this meeting as she had not had the opportunity to be close to him during the week. She let her hair down and put on a pretty dress, one that was low-cut so it would be easier for Ewan to touch her breasts. She couldn't wait to feel his hands on her naked skin, especially her secret parts. She had thought about that electric feeling that ran through her body when this happened. Then for a moment her mind went back to Edward and their night together; she knew she had egged him on a little but that was only to help him overcome his stuffiness. She had not seen him since then. She hoped she hadn't upset him too much, as she had told him so many truths about himself.

As she made her way to Ewan's cottage she skipped

along like a schoolgirl on her way to school. She could see him in the distance and he looked so handsome. He was wearing a white T-shirt and she could see his taut biceps. I love you so much, Ewan, please love me back, she whispered to herself as she neared his cottage. "Hi, Emmeline," he called and held his arms out for her to come to him. She nestled into his broad shoulders and held him tight. "I've been waiting to be in your arms, Ewan, I feel so happy and safe, I want to stay here forever. Please don't let me go, ever," she pleaded with him. "You are my girl, Emmeline, I will love and care for you. Let us stroll along the lake's edge and enjoy the smell and the moods of the lake." He let her go from his arms and took her hand and away they went. He stooped to pick up stones and skip them across the water, sometimes managing ten skips. She loved watching him flex his muscles and had an urge to touch them and feel their tautness, so she reached up and squeezed them. "Come, Emmeline, I will race you back to the cottage," and away he ran. He had strong powerful strides and she was left in his dust. "Wait for me," she called, but he was gone. She sat down and tears came to her eyes. Did he not want her to touch him, because when she did he ran away. Ewan looked back and saw her on the ground, so he came running back, then he noticed her tears. "What's wrong, Emmeline, did you hurt yourself?" Could she tell him what she thought? "I thought you ran away because I touched your body." "You silly girl, I wanted us to get back to the cottage so we could be together in private." With that he picked her up in his arms and strode back to his home.

He made a cup of tea and they sat at the table as he had made some scones. He wanted to have a serious talk with her about one of the new men at the collieries. She had to know. When he told her, she was not happy. "Do you think my uncles are behind this?" she asked. "I'm picking that is what is going on; apparently there is talk among the men and they are worried in case they have to work for them." "They will never get the collieries, Ewan. Papa told me not to let them have them, he knew what would happen." He told her he had warned the miner if it happened again he would have to go, as the miners' safety was paramount.

She thanked Ewan for keeping her up to date and went over to him and led him to the settee. They sat down and she snuggled into him, then that feeling came back, the one that appeared whenever their bodies were close to each other. She didn't have to put his hand on her bare skin, he put it there himself. Once he started to caress her she became aroused and begged him to touch her more. He didn't know what she meant; surely she didn't want him to touch other parts of her body. With that she stood up and undid her dress and let it fall to the floor, then she undid her bodice and stood naked from the waist up. He stared at her bare breasts, they were firm and beautiful; he pulled her to him and kissed them. "Ewan, take your shirt off, I want to feel your bare skin next to mine." He stood up and pulled off his T-shirt and led her through to his bedroom. They lay on the bed together in each other's arms with their bare skin touching. He kissed her passionately and she pulled him hard against her. "I have never done anything like this before, Ewan, I know there is more, I want more," she begged. He told her he would not go any further as he wanted her to think seriously about the consequences. Deep down he wanted it as much as she did, but he had to think of her position. She was a very wealthy heiress, he was of lower standing than her.

"Emmeline, I will never take advantage of you or your position. You are wealthy, I don't have much to offer you other than love, but will that be enough?" "Love is all I want from you, Ewan, of course it is enough. I want to give you my body completely." With this confession, she held him close and they lay in each other's arms and drifted off to sleep.

Sometime during the night, they were woken by the town siren. This spelt disaster at a colliery. They both jumped out of bed, dressed and ran to the door. People were gathering in the village square, so they both ran to Emmeline's stables and hitched the cart to the horses and drove to the coal-pit. The lights were bright and men were gathering at the shaft entrance. Ewan ran over and learned that something had happened down in the shaft. He got into the emergency cage and asked to be let down, which was strictly against the rules; no one was meant to enter until it was clear what had happened. When he reached the shaft, there were men staggering everywhere and three men were lying unconscious on the ground. He lifted the unconscious men into the cage and propped them up and told the men that were struggling to breathe to get into the cage with them, and they were pulled to the surface. The rest would go up when the cage came back.

He ran down to the barometer station and was gutted to find it had reach the critical mark. This meant the methane gas reading was too high, causing the breathing problems. These men should not have been down in the shafts, they should have evacuated before it got to this level. When it reached high this was the evacuation point but it had gone past high, past danger to critical. It could not have reached this level in one hour, it would have taken at least three hours to climb this high. Someone had not been checking the barometer! Ewan checked that all men were accounted for, then he went up in the final cage.

Emmeline was with the onsite medic making sure that the men were going to be okay. She worried about Ewan being down there, then she thought back to what he had told her earlier in the night, about the miner from her uncles' colliery. When he emerged she ran to him. Together they walked back to see that all the men were safe. The three unconscious men were now conscious but would not be fit for work for a few days. Emmeline assured them that they were not to return until they were well, and their pay packets would continue. The rest of the men were sent home and would be notified when it was safe for them to re-enter the shafts. Ewan saw the culprit trying to sneak off, so he grabbed him by the scruff of his neck and dragged him back into his office. Emmeline followed them in. She remembered this young man. Ewan said to him, "I warned you about checking the barometer each hour, you have put all the men's lives in danger because of your stupidity. You are finished, don't let me see you near this coal-pit ever again. Now get out!" and he shoved him out the door. "This is the start, Emmeline, your uncles are determined to get your collieries, we must be careful! They have probably offered these men good jobs when they take over. You go home, I will stay and check the gas levels in the shafts." "Please be careful, we have unfinished business," she lovingly whispered to him. She walked over to the cart and climbed on and took the reins and guided the horses back to the stables. It was four o'clock in the morning when she climbed into bed.

Jane woke Miss Emmeline as Mr Stenhouse was waiting for her in the drawing room; he had come as soon as he had heard there was trouble at her collieries. She quickly dressed and went to meet him. This was the first time they had seen each other after their night out. He still felt upset with himself over what had happened, so what did he do, he started with an apology. "Mr Stenhouse, Edward, we made a new rule: no negatives, only positives; forget the apologies, we had a good night out. How can I help you?" He stood and looked at Emmeline and smiled; she couldn't believe how different he looked when he smiled. "Now that's what I like to see," she let him know. "I was worried when I heard something had happen in your collieries, what happened, what went wrong?" Emmeline explained the problem and the cause. "We will wait and see because I think my uncles will come back with an offer, but they will never get Papa's collieries. I know you will help me make sure this never happens, Edward, sorry, Mr Stenhouse." He smiled again and assured her he was her accountant and had her interests at heart ... in his heart! She put her hand out to shake his and he bent down and kissed it. "That is sweet, Edward," she said and they both laughed, remembering this very same thing happening on their night out. "Take care, Emmeline."

14

Is Something in the Air?

Meanwhile, Jane was worried as Miss Emmeline had been spending a lot of time at Mr Ewan Thomas Fletcher's cottage. She had an uneasy feeling; Thomas, did this name have any significance? He was very much involved with the welfare of the mining industry and Miss Emmeline had told her he was going to present something to the Parliament, to make a better life for the miners. Could this be the 'Thomas' that Mr Christian mentioned? He had all the credentials to be Mr Christian's illegitimate son. She knew his family lived in Cockermouth, Miss Emmeline had told her so. She had Quaker friends that lived there, perhaps they could help her look into his background. How tragic for Miss Emmeline if Ewan was indeed her half-brother. She would have to get on to this right away before their relationship developed too far. Little did she know how far it had developed. If this was so, how would Jane tell her? She would ask for a couple of days off and travel to Cockermouth by train.

Emmeline went to the coal-pit mid-morning to speak to Ewan to find out how the men were. He hadn't been to bed, he had stayed at the office to make sure nothing else went wrong. "Emmeline, I have spoken to some of the men to find out who the second 'nark' is but they will not break their silence. It is a vulnerable situation for them as accidents happen so easily underground, if they give out a name there is sure to be retaliation. We will have to monitor this with the upmost care until we find our man, as there is sure to be another disruption. That is what they were put here to do." "Please, Ewan, go home and get some sleep, I will stay until you get back. When do you think it will be safe for the men to go back to work?" "I will check later this afternoon and if all is well, we can start the night shift at twelve o'clock. Thanks, Emmeline, I will get some sleep." She told him to take her cart home and bring it back later. Her kissed her goodbye and left. She would stay until he returned. Some of the men had come in to see when it was safe for them to return to work, as they were worried about having the time docked off their pay. She assured them that because it was a workplace accident, they would receive full pay.

While she was sitting at Ewan's desk, she noticed he had several envelopes neatly addressed to the Parliament. She wondered if he had finished his thesis and was ready to put submissions forward for a new mining bill to protect the miners. Emmeline felt terrible as she had not discussed much about his thesis lately. Perhaps she had been selfish and was consumed in her own little world? Her mind went back to her papa; he would have approved of Ewan and what he was doing for the miners. She wished they had met. She would ask him to come with her one day to visit her papa's gravesite up on the hill. This was where she had first set eyes on Ewan; would he remember this? The rest of the day passed slowly, as the men were waiting to hear when they could go back to work. When Ewan arrived back, he went straight down the shaft to read the barometer, and the reading was back to normal. This meant the night shift could start at twelve o'clock. He put the word out to the miners.

The next morning, Jane asked Miss Emmeline if she could take a couple of days off as she had a sick aunt she had to visit in Cockermouth; could she leave tomorrow? This was fine by her. Jane could hardly look Miss Emmeline in the eye as she never told lies, let alone told untruths to her employer. She valued her job and Mr Christian had been very good to her mother and herself. She cared dearly for Miss Emmeline and didn't want to see her hurt, but she did wonder what lay ahead: was it heartache and pain?

Emmeline's groundsman had spent the past week at the homes of the widows preparing their garden plots and planting vegetable plants. Emmeline had asked for the rose bushes to be planted at the front door of each cottage, so they would be seen each time they entered or exited their homes, be it in remembrance of a lost loved one. Later that afternoon when school had finished, Emmeline received a visit from Desmond and little John. They were going to walk to the farmlet to see how the animals were. "Don't walk, take the cart. Would you mind if I came with you?" she asked. They were both delighted. "We don't see you much any more, Miss Emmeline," said little John. "I'm sorry, I have been busy, but I will make more time for you.

I have missed you both." As they rode to the farmlet, little John said he was going to his granny's for a week of the school holidays. She asked Desmond if he was going but he had school books to mark over the school break. "You must bring me a photo of your granny when you come back," she requested.

When they arrived, there were lots of children; some were feeding the piglets scraps, others were looking for eggs and two mothers were milking the cows. The sheep had arrived and were grazing, everything looked really good. It wasn't going to be long and they would have an extra couple of babies to care for as the cows' bellies had certainly grown. She had brought another bucket of wheat for the chooks, and this had to do them a week; the children knew this. She spoke with the mothers to see how they were managing and they were happy and thanked her for her kind donations for their gardens. Emmeline asked if they would contact the other widows and she would hold a meeting at the farmlet next Thursday at two o'clock.

Desmond and Emmeline stood and watched as little John played with the other children, telling them about going to the market to buy the animals. Desmond was unusually quiet today, so she asked him what was wrong. It was three years ago to the day that his wife was taken from him. She didn't know what had happened as he hadn't spoken about it. "What went wrong, Desmond?" He had tears in his eyes and told her she had died in childbirth along with the baby. She put her arms around him to comfort him. "That must have been terrible to lose them both." "Yes, it was so sad, we were looking forward to building our family, now there is only little John and myself. I am still trying to get over it, Emmeline. As I told you when you lost your papa, time heals, but there are certain days when things come flooding back and this is one of them." She stood with her arms around him. Little John came over and asked her if she loved his daddy. "Yes, little John, you have a wonderful daddy. Would you both like to come and have supper with me tonight?" "Please, can we, Daddy, please say yes?" he pleaded. They said goodbye to everyone at the farmlet, climbed on to the cart and drove back to the stables.

Desmond unhitched the horses and Emmeline and little John brought some hay over to feed them. "You have lots of things, are you rich, Miss Emmeline?" he asked. "No, not really, but I am comfortable and I'm happy, that is the main thing, to be happy." With this she thought of Ewan. They walked up to her home and she asked Jane to make supper for three. Little John asked if he could see all of her big home, so they went on a grand tour.

They started in the drawing room, then the library; he had never seen so many books, they were stacked in shelves nearly to the sky, he told her. Next, they went into her papa's office and little John ran to the big chair and sat in it. "This is a big desk, who sits here?" Emmeline explained it was her papa's, this was where he did all his business, but now that he was gone it was her desk. "Come and sit in this chair, Daddy," he called. Desmond went and sat in the chair. "That suits you, you look good behind that desk, doesn't he, little John?" "Perhaps Daddy might sit here one day?" he said innocently. They laughed and carried on upstairs to the bedrooms, five in all, and two bathrooms and toilets. "This is a very big home; are you scared on your own, Miss Emmeline?" She told him that Jane lived here with her at the moment. With that Jane called them to say supper was served in the dining room.

The three of them sat at the big dining table and

chattered away as they ate. "I'm looking forward to my holiday with my granny," said little John. "Where does she live?" asked Emmeline. "Where is it, Daddy, is it Whitehaven? Yes, it is Whitehaven, I remember. She is a nice lady and spoils me." "And so she should, you deserve to be spoilt," remarked Emmeline. After they had eaten, Desmond suggested they take a walk by the lake. The three of them walked hand in hand with little John in the middle; he loved it when he could hold Miss Emmeline's hand and his daddy's.

At the same time, Desmond's cousin Mr Stenhouse was coming along the road in his carriage; he had been to a meeting. When he saw the three of them holding hands and laughing, he wished it was him that was there with Miss Emmeline with their child. This was the first time he had even considered another person other than him and Miss Emmeline. He loved her so much; of course she would want children. She made him happy, he had never laughed so much, or had such fun as he did on their night out together. She wasn't frightened to tell him what she was thinking, she was truthful in a sort of tender way, with how she put things. He had stopped putting his food into little piles on his plate; she was right, he was organised and stuffy. He was going to change. He had even been to town and bought some casual clothes, as he wanted to look more like George. He had to admit, George looked much younger than him; he hadn't noticed until Miss Emmeline had told him so.

The three of them waved to Mr Stenhouse so he pulled up in his carriage and dismounted. He walked over and greeted them and to Emmeline's surprise he even acknowledged little John by giving him a penny; this was a first. "Thank you, Mr Edward, I will spend it on my holiday," he said. "Can we sit down? My legs are tired." "That's a good idea," replied Emmeline. She was interested to see how Mr Stenhouse would handle this situation. To her surprise he sat down on the little pebble bank and joined in.

He and Desmond talked about family, and she and little John talked about his holiday. She asked him not to forget the photo of him with his grandma. He was getting tired so he cuddled into Emmeline and she put her arms around him. Mr Stenhouse looked on and imagined he was his and Emmeline's own little boy, that this was his family. How proud he would be. But it was just a dream and would never be anything else, as she wasn't interested in him. He offered to take them home in his carriage, and for this little John was pleased.

When they pulled up at Desmond's home, Emmeline got out with them and gave little John a big hug and said to him, "Have a nice holiday." She put her arms around Desmond and held on to him, as she knew it had been a sad day for him, then she kissed him on the cheek and said goodbye. Instead of getting angry being a witness to all this, Mr Stenhouse closed his eyes and imagined this was happening to him; it made him happier to imagine it was him and Miss Emmeline. After the goodbyes she climbed onto the seat next to him and asked if he would drop her at her home. Of course, any excuse to get close to her. She told him that Jane had asked for a few days off and was leaving tomorrow. "Will you be all right on your own?" he enquired. "Yes, don't forget I am seventeen now, I can handle myself, that you are well aware of," and with this they both laughed. "Yes, you certainly say what you are thinking. I want to tell you I no longer play with my food any more; my eating stuffiness has gone, thanks to you." "Mr Stenhouse, you are changing for the better. If you keep this up you will meet a nice young lady one day who will appreciate you." "But I have already met ..." then he stopped before he made a fool of himself. "You were saying?" Emmeline wanted him to finish what he was saying. Had he met someone already? She was dying to know, but silence fell. Was this why he was changing — to impress a lady friend? She hadn't noticed his twitches lately, perhaps the change was agreeing with him.

They pulled up at the entrance to her home and he jumped down and rushed around to help her down. "This is a bit different to the last time we pulled up here, it was me rushing around to help you, but you were beyond help," she laughed. Poor Mr Stenhouse, he put his head down in shame. "It's all right, Edward, I'm having a joke with you, you are so easily offended," and she lifted his head. "Don't take things to heart; remember, be positive," and she gave him a peck on his cheek and ran inside. He still needed reassurance, but she would work on this. Little did she realise that with every smidgen of kindness she gave to him, the deeper his love became for her.

Jane left early the next morning to go to visit her sick aunt in Cockermouth. Ewan had asked Emmeline to come to his office as he had several miners applying for the new miner's job and he wanted her to make the decision. She decided to pick a man on his merit and forget about helping out her uncles' men, as that had nearly caused a disaster in her collieries, besides there was still a 'nark' at her coal-pit. After interviewing the men, she chose one who had a young family to provide for, as they were the ones that needed the money most, and she knew the children would be fed. She asked Ewan if he would like to come to her home and stay, seeing Jane was away, as she hadn't been there at night on her own before. Of course he agreed; he didn't want her there on her own if she didn't feel comfortable. He would come around after he had finished work, but first he would go to his cottage and pick up some clothes. Emmeline was so happy, she couldn't wait until tonight. She would ask Ewan to sleep with her in her big bed and she would cuddle into him and feel his naked body. She had never seen a naked man before, just the drawings in the journal she found in her papa's desk. She had seen plenty of nude girls at boarding school, but male bodies had not been discussed, probably because none of the other girls had seen a naked man either.

When Mr Stenhouse closed his office, he decided to call on Miss Emmeline on his way home as he had had a visit from her uncles. He knocked at her door and waited. As the door was opened, there before him stood a vision of beauty. Emmeline had let her hair down and put on a pretty dress, all for Ewan's benefit. So she was quite shocked to see Mr Stenhouse standing there. "You look pretty, Miss Emmeline, may I come in? I had a visit from your uncles this afternoon," he said politely. She was not prepared for this visit and really wanted him to leave before Ewan arrived. "Could I come to your office in the morning, as I have visitors coming?" He wondered who might be visiting her, but apologised and took his leave.

As he was getting down the road he could see Mr Fletcher coming towards him with an overnight bag. Surely this wasn't Miss Emmeline's visitor; why was he carrying an overnight bag? As he got closer he noticed he was showered, as his hair was still wet and he looked fresh and tidy. As Mr Fletcher passed Mr Stenhouse he greeted him. "Good evening." He watched where he went, and yes, he was heading straight for Miss Emmeline's home. He wouldn't be staying with her, he couldn't be. Jane would never allow this to happen while she was in the house. He couldn't get this image out of his head, and the more he thought about it, the more jealous he became. He needed a good stiff whisky, perhaps even two, three ... Surely Miss Emmeline would not let this stranger touch any part of her body; she would feel so soft, and he dreamt on and on ... He had never had sexual thoughts but the closer he became to Miss Emmeline, the stronger they became. Then suddenly he remembered Jane was going to visit a sick relative so Miss Emmeline was at home on her own, so she and Mr Fletcher were going to be in the stately home together. That was why he was carrying an overnight bag. Where was he going to sleep? The whiskies were taking effect and all too soon it was him in bed with Miss Emmeline ...

Emmeline had cooked Ewan supper, they had eaten and cleaned up the dishes. They went to the drawing room and relaxed and talked about their new miner. She told him Mr Stenhouse had called to say that her uncles had approached him with another offer. They were going to discuss it tomorrow. Ewan didn't mention about seeing him on his way to her home. As bedtime approached, Ewan asked which room was his so he could put his bag there. "I want you to share my bed, Ewan, I want us to bed together tonight." "But Emmeline, I didn't expect this to happen. I thought you wanted me to stay so you wouldn't be here on your own." He told her he didn't think she realised the consequences of two people sleeping together and she wasn't ready for this to happen, it was too soon. "That I touch your breasts and caress you is where it starts and ends. I really want you, but now is not the time. I love you, Emmeline, but respect must prevail here. Don't be upset, we can lie together and caress each other, but we will not be sharing a bed for the night. Emmeline's dream was not going to be realised tonight but she was happy with where they were at. She ran her hands down his arms and on to his chest, he was so strong, and she continued down to his waist. She wanted to go further but Ewan brought her hand back to his chest. He decided to call it a night as he could see it was going to get out of hand. He kissed her goodnight and went to his own room and shut the door.

He woke around seven o'clock and make some breakfast then walked to the coal-pit, as he didn't want to disturb Emmeline. When she woke she tiptoed to his bedroom but he was gone. She put her hair into braids and went downstairs to make some breakfast, before she left for her appointment with Mr Stenhouse. As soon as she arrived at his office she was shown straight through, as he was eagerly awaiting her. "Come in, Miss Emmeline, did you have a nice night last night?" he asked. "Yes, as a matter of fact I had a great night." What a strange thing for him to ask, she thought. This was not what he wanted to hear, anything else, but not this. "What did my uncles offer this time?" she asked. "They had heard about the near disaster at your collieries and don't think you are capable of running them. They want me to persuade you to let them have a lease. They are prepared to pay you good money for the royalties, but Mr Fletcher has to go, as he would not be part of the deal." "If it wasn't for their planted 'nark' this would not have happened at my collieries, and of course they don't want Ewan, he would protect the men and they wouldn't want that. They want to exploit the miners and work them harder. No way will

I allow this to happen; I hope I have your backing?" He could see that this would be one way to get rid of Mr Fletcher from Emmeline's life, but if it backfired she might give him a more permanent position ... as her husband! "I will back you all the way, the collieries are working well and making plenty of money, in fact you are very wealthy, and the men respect you. I will tell your uncles not to come back with any more offers, you are not for lease or sale!" "Thank you for supporting me on this, you will be rewarded." But would she reward him in the way he wanted? He could still see a tiny smidgen of hope, though it be very faint, but where there was a will, there was a way, that was positive thinking! As she stood up to leave, she put her hand out to shake his and he held on to it; it felt soft and warm as it always did, then he bent down and kissed it. "You are sweet, Edward" were her parting words. She was thinking he did have a lady friend, as he had changed, and she would ask him one day.

It was Thursday and Jane was due back today, so Ewan took his overnight bag to work this morning. Just after lunch there was a knock at her door and when she opened it there stood her uncles. She invited them into the parlour but they wanted to go to her papa's office for a meeting. She sat in her papa's chair and let them talk. Mr Stenhouse had told them that she wanted no more offers on her collieries, that they were not for lease. "That's right, I gave him those instructions. They will never be for lease. Papa wanted me to run them and that's what I am going to do." "But Emmeline, you are already a very wealthy young lady; we have no income, will you not let us pay you a royalty, so we can make some money?" they asked. "I'm sorry, uncles, but you ran your colliery different to my father." "Yes, we know, Emmeline, but they could be so much more productive if the men were made to work harder. Your father was too kind to the men, he treated them as friends, not as workers." "Yes, I know, and I will do the same; we have no unrest or strikes because the miners are happy. I am not going to change my mind, you will have to look elsewhere to lease," she told them sternly. "You may be sorry for this decision, Emmeline." "Don't threaten me, I will mention this to Mr Fletcher, he will not be happy," she said. "Oh yes, he would be the first to go, who does he think he is, hassling our man?" This confirmed to Emmeline that the 'nark' worked for them. She told them to leave immediately and not to bother coming back. She had thought they may have supported her, as her papa was their brother, but this was not so; they were greedy men with no scruples and now they were desperate.

Emmeline was so angry she hitched the horses to the cart and drove to the coal-pit. She told Ewan the full conversation; he was worried as threats had been made. Emmeline saw the envelopes were still on his desk and asked him about them. Yes, they were his thesis and were ready to be posted or taken to a member of the House. Then they had to go before a committee of the House of Commons, where it was considered before it could proceed to legislate on the matter. She asked him if he wanted to take a couple of days so he could deliver it personally. "I had thought of delivering it myself, then I would know it had reached them. There is nothing to say they will pass it as a bill, but I will have done my best for the miners and for their safety." "Go tomorrow, Ewan, catch the train, get it to them before there are any more colliery disasters. I will pay your expenses as this is going to benefit the miners, it will be a workplace expense." He refused her money and said he wanted to fund it himself. "I will go tomorrow; will you take my place here until I get back?" he asked. Emmeline agreed, so that was settled. He showed her what had to be done over the next couple of days, and she had to be there for any complaints that might come in from the miners. Ewan wanted to get back as soon as possible in case any problems arose. They said their goodbyes and she wish him luck, as she would not be seeing him in the morning.

On the way home she decided to call and see how Desmond was getting on without little John as he had started his holiday with his granny. She hitched the horses to the gate post and knocked at his door. Desmond was surprised to see Emmeline standing there and invited her in. He apologised for the mess, as he had children's books scattered all over his table. "I've just come to see how you are coping without your little boy. Are you missing him?" He said he missed his questions and funny little sayings, as they made him laugh. "You know, Emmeline, if I didn't have him, my life would be worth nothing. I'm so happy I have you as a friend; we share similar likes, we are dreamers, whether they come true or not, one just has to hold on to them. One thing about dreams, they can change with every moment." "You are so right, Desmond, I never thought of that. They are not a permanent thing, they are floating thoughts that come and go. If one dream doesn't come true, we move on to another. Not everyone would understand that, but you and I do."

Desmond put the kettle on. Then he asked how everything was going at her collieries, so she told him what was happening and the threats from her uncles. She told him Ewan was away to present his thesis to the House of Commons. He told her if she needed any help with anything to let him know, especially where the uncles were concerned. "Thank you, Desmond, you are a very dear friend. Come for supper tomorrow night, I want you to help me sort out Papa's office." They said their goodbyes with a hug.

When Emmeline arrived home, Jane was already back. "How was your aunt?" she asked. Jane told her that she was getting better as she busied herself, not wanting to face Miss Emmeline with having told her a lie. Jane said she had a nice time but it was good to be back. "How is Mr Fletcher?" she asked. Emmeline told Jane she was deeply in love with him and he loved her too. She was so excited she wanted to tell her she had let him touch her breasts, but she thought better. "Miss Emmeline, you may think you are in love with Mr Fletcher but what do you know about his background?" "Does it really matter? He told me his mother used to live around here. He doesn't know much about his father, but his mother remarried and shifted to Cockermouth as that was where her new husband worked. He has three half siblings who are much younger than him. His mother had money so she was able to give him an education." Was there money given to the lady with the little boy who came that day to visit Mr Christian? Perhaps it was for his education; was this Thomas, Mr Christian's illegitimate son? Jane had tried to see Mr Fletcher's mother while she was at Cockermouth to see if she recognised her, but alas, this was not to be. She hoped Emmeline had not let Mr Fletcher touch her; imagine if he was her half-brother. She was sure she had solved the mystery. In the meantime, she would keep her eye on Emmeline and Mr Fletcher.

The next day had come to an end and as Emmeline was finishing at the office, one of the miners that she had hired from her uncles' colliery came in. He wanted to know where Mr Fletcher lived as he wanted to speak to him away from the coal-pit. She gave him Ewan's address thinking he may want to speak to him about the 'nark'. She went and said goodbye to the night staff before she left. Then she remembered she had asked Desmond for supper so had to let Jane know. Jane was much more receptive to this friendship. It wasn't that she disliked Mr Fletcher but it was the unknown that worried her. She still had relatives searching for more information on Mr Ewan Thomas Fletcher.

When Desmond arrived, he and Emmeline went into her papa's office. "Desmond, Papa has all these papers here and I don't know if they are important or whether I can throw them away. I thought you might know what to keep!" Desmond said he would look through them and sort them out. He put them in separate piles as he went. He knew all the tax papers had to be kept as well as the financials that had come from Mr Stenhouse's office, but there were so may receipts that weren't needed, just the current ones. He found a couple of envelopes marked private so he gave them to Emmeline to read. She sat down and opened them. The first one was the purchase of land surrounding the collieries and the application to start them. It had a map of the areas that Mr Christian had purchased, and she was surprised to see that it included the colliery that the uncles owned. Had her papa given the land to them? If so, they had little to complain about. She would show these to Mr Stenhouse, he might know. The second letter contained a receipt for a large amount of money, described as school fees for Thomas. It gave no evidence to whom it was paid or even a school that may have received it. This brought tears to Emmeline's eyes; this almost confirmed that Thomas was her father's son, her half-brother! Where would she find him? She took the letter to Jane to read as she knew about Thomas. Jane fought to hide her tears as now it almost confirmed what she was thinking. Mr Fletcher was Mr Christian's illegitimate son; how would she tell Miss Emmeline? She loved him! It wasn't the right time yet, but it would have to be dealt with soon.

Desmond was busy sorting through the papers when Jane brought supper in for him and Emmeline. She thought Desmond was the right one for Miss Emmeline; they seemed more suited, now that she knew about Mr Fletcher. Once Emmeline knew the truth she would turn to Desmond, he would be her rock, and she loved little John. They sat and ate supper while he kept sorting the papers, as there were certainly plenty of piles to attend to. Several hours later he had the desk and draws cleaned out, and the relevant papers that needed to be kept were filed away. What a difference! Desmond told her he would come any time she wanted things sorted, she just had to ask. Emmeline was very thankful and offered to pay him for the hours he had spent at the desk. He adamantly refused saying they were very good friends and friends helped each other. As it was very late they hitched the horses to the carriage and Emmeline drove him home.

A couple of days had gone by and Emmeline really missed Ewan; she was hoping he would come home today, as tomorrow, being Friday, was their special day. She looked forward to going to Ewan's cottage for all the wonderful memories it held. Her wish was granted as he arrived back at the coal-pit office just as she was finishing for the day. They embraced each other and she was excited to hear all about the House of Commons. Ewan was tired and just wanted to fall into bed and catch up on some sleep, so they arranged to meet at his cottage after work tomorrow.

Today being Friday, Emmeline decided to take one of the papers marked private that came from her papa's desk to Mr Stenhouse to clarify if in fact her papa had given the land to her uncles. She also wanted to tell him they threatened her. As always, she was most welcome at Mr Stenhouse's office. As he read the papers, he was surprised to find that Emmeline's papa had not only given the uncles the land, he had, in fact, given them the colliery. He had set it all up for them and then verbally gifted it to them. So, what they owned was not of their own doing, it was a gift from their brother, and now they wanted his other two collieries.

As Mr Stenhouse explained the papers to her, they were both surprised to learn of this. "You know, I am so angry with them. They visited me after you told them not to come back with any more offers and had the cheek to threaten me if I didn't lease to them. I told them to leave and not to bother coming back. What ungrateful men." Mr Stenhouse was upset to think they had threatened Miss Emmeline, their own niece, but desperation drove people to take desperate measures. He would keep his eye out for these two men. He told her if they came near her again to contact him.

Emmeline went home after her visit to his office. She talked with Jane and told her not to worry about supper for her tonight as she was going to visit Mr Fletcher. "What time will you be back, Miss Emmeline?" Jane asked. This was an unusual request from Jane; she had never asked her before. "Probably late, so don't wait up for me." Jane was alarmed with this answer; should she tell her the truth now or let her have one more date with him? She decided on the latter. Tomorrow would be the day Miss Emmeline's life would change forever ... but she had to know!

15

Will the Truth
be Revealed?

Emmeline spent the rest of the afternoon washing and brushing her hair to have it pretty for Ewan. She would put ribbons in so as to look special. She had bought a nice new bodice so that when she dropped her dress she would look inviting. She was so excited. Perhaps tonight Ewan might want to lie naked beside her in bed! As she was leaving, Jane called out to her. "Enjoy yourself tonight, Miss Emmeline." Again, she was surprised by Jane's concern for her; what was going on?

She made her way down to Ewan's cottage but when she arrived he was not at home. She decided to take a walk along the lake hoping he would be back soon. This was the first time in months she had taken the time to think about her heroine and Belle Isle. She sat down and took a moment or two to focus back on how their two lives were now starting to differ. Isabella had her two cousins as her suitors, she had Ewan. With that thought she was interrupted by a voice calling her name. She looked up and could see her man in the distance. She ran along the lake front and into his outstretched arms. They sat out on the porch while Ewan explained all about his train trip to London. He had met with the relevant authorities, now it was a waiting game. They were impressed with his thesis and his recommendations for a new bill to be passed to protect the safety of the miners. Emmeline was so proud of him, he was special ... he was her man! He had bought supper from the colliery store so they went inside to eat. She kept him up to date with what had been happening while he was away. She didn't know whether to tell him about the letter marked private that was on her papa's desk that almost confirmed she had a half-brother. Probably better to leave it tonight; she would tell him one day.

Ewan took her hand and led her to the settee where they sat and kissed passionately. He put his hand gently on her breast, and he could feel her heart starting to beat faster. Emmeline stood up and led him to his bedroom. She undid her dress and let it slip to the floor. He noticed her new bodice and commented how nice it looked, then came over and untied it. This was the first time he had removed an article of her clothing. He cupped her breasts in his hands and kissed and caressed them. She was so excited she stepped back and dropped her petticoat and slipped down her knickers, and stood stark naked in front of Ewan. She was beautiful. He just stood and gazed at her young firm body; he had not expected this to happen. He was totally taken by surprise.

She lay down on his bed and asked him to touch her whole body. Where was this leading? He felt she was not ready for what she wanted to happen. He was worried as had she ever seen a naked man; what would she expect to see? He knelt on the floor and touched her body to her waist. He was reluctant to touch any lower; his body was aching to take her, but something told him to hold back. She took his hand and put it on her other secret part. He looked at Emmeline; she was so innocent, did she really know what she wanted, did she know the consequences? There were so many questions, but very few answers. He stood up and covered her from the waist down. "What's wrong, Ewan, don't you like my body, is something wrong?" "There is nothing wrong, you are beautiful, Emmeline, but first we must talk about this." "Do you know the difference between a man and a woman?" and with this she hesitated. "Do you know what happens to a man when he lies next to a naked lady?" he asked. Emmeline didn't know. She had never talked about sex with anyone, so she told him this. He told her to get up and put her petticoat and knickers back on. Emmeline reluctantly did as Ewan asked. He was happy to touch and kiss her breasts, this she was ready for, but the rest was not going to be a happening thing. He took off his top and they lay together with their bare upper bodies touching.

Suddenly they were disturbed with the sound of breaking glass. Ewan jumped up and opened his bedroom door only to see something had been thrown through his window. He told Emmeline to get dressed and to stay in the bedroom. She pleaded for him to stay with her, but there were men outside yelling for him to come out. He didn't want them to come in and hurt Emmeline, so he went out. As he stepped out the door he felt a blow to his head, then nothing as he fell to the ground. All was quiet so she went to the door and saw two men bending over Ewan. She recognised them from the collieries; when they saw her they were in shock, and panicked and took off. Emmeline was not part of the equation. Now they had been seen and recognised, what were they going to do? They weren't meant to kill him, just rough him up.

She bent down but Ewan was out to it. She called his name but there was no response. What would she do? She couldn't leave him on his own, so she lifted his head and lay it on her lap. It was only then she noticed he was bleeding profusely from his head. She started to cry, then she screamed for help. Neighbours heard the scream and came running. They were shocked when they saw Ewan; they knew then that it was too late, but Emmeline had no idea. She was still crying and cuddling him. The lady came over and lifted Ewan's head off her lap and lay him on the ground. She lifted her up and took her in her arms and turned her away. Emmeline was devastated, but she knew he would get better. The man had gone into the cottage and brought a blanket out and laid it over Ewan. When Emmeline saw this, she fell to her knees, her heart was broken. He wasn't going to get better. The lady asked her where she lived and walked her home.

Jane had been waiting for Miss Emmeline to return and when she heard the knock at the door she panicked. She opened it and was greeted by a strange lady holding Miss Emmeline in her arms. She was covered in blood. What had happened? The lady explained what they had been confronted with and that the young man had been killed. As soon as Emmeline heard that Ewan had been killed she let out a scream; she didn't want to believe it, but in her heart, she knew it was true. Jane thanked the lady and took Miss Emmeline inside. She walked with her up the stairs to her room, then lay her on the bed and put a cover over her. She lay beside her — she would clean her up later — listening to her sobbing for Ewan, repeating his name over and over again. When Emmeline finally dropped off to sleep, Jane went down to the medicine cabinet and found some tranquilisers, just in case they were needed.

Jane went into the parlour and sat down on her chair and put her head in her hands. She thought back to earlier in the night, when she made the decision not to tell Miss Emmeline about Mr Fletcher, to give her one more night with him; now the secret would never have to be revealed! But what had happened to him? The lady said he had been killed, someone must have done this. She went back upstairs to Miss Emmeline's room and sat in her chair, just to keep an eye on her.

Jane must have dropped off to sleep, as when she woke the sun was shining in the room and Miss Emmeline was gone. She jumped up and ran through the home calling her name but to no avail. She noticed her bloodstained dress on the bathroom floor, and stood for a moment wondering where she might be. She went upstairs to the attic window and looked down to the lake. She could see a lonely figure sitting on the bank. This was where she went when her papa passed away. Jane stood and watched her. She had experienced such heartache for someone so young; thank God she was spared one last heartache! This would never be revealed, it would go to the grave with Ewan.

Today was Saturday and Desmond had woken early and decided to walk along the lake; he didn't have little John to worry about, because he was still holidaying with his granny. He remembered his first walk, when they had bumped into a young lady sitting by the lake crying. He thanked his lucky stars that he had met Emmeline that day, otherwise she might never have been part of their lives. Today was overcast and the lake looked angry; it was kicking up its heels making white tops, warning that it didn't want to be messed with. As he walked past the place he had first met Emmeline, he looked up only to see her sitting in the same place sobbing. He quickly walked up to her. "Emmeline, is something wrong? What has happened?" She couldn't tell him anything; all she could do was sob. He put his arms around her and she responded by cuddling into him, but she still could not talk. Desmond said nothing, he was there to comfort her, to get her through whatever had happened.

Two hours had passed and still not a word had been spoken, but she needed him to be with her. His shirt was wet with her tears, but he knew something terrible had happened. He saw the funeral carriage coming up the street from down by the lake, but at this time he didn't know Mr Fletcher lived there. Perhaps this was someone Emmeline knew. When she did manage to stop crying for one moment, all she could say was Ewan's name over and over again. Surely something hadn't happened to him? "Emmeline, tell me what's wrong?" "I've lost Ewan. Two men came around to his cottage last night and hit him over the head, they killed him," she sobbed. "Oh, I'm so sorry, you will feel it is the end of the world, but it's not, Emmeline." He knew only too well what she was going through. He held her closer and hoped his arms were a safe haven for her at this moment in time.

Things slowly came back to Emmeline as to what had happened the previous night, although she was she was still deeply distraught. The police were at her home asking questions. Did she see the men? Why were they there? Why would they want to harm Mr Fletcher? She told them the men were employed at her collieries, but they didn't belong there because they would not follow the safety procedures. She didn't mention that they were employed at her uncles' colliery before coming to her. Suddenly Emmeline burst into tears; she remembered that one of the men was the one that had come to her office and asked for Ewan's address, and she had given it to him. Was she responsible for Ewan's death? She felt sick inside. She excused herself and ran upstairs to her room, lay on her bed and sobbed until there were no tears left. Jane went up and covered her and left her to try to work her way forward. She was heartbroken for Miss Emmeline, but there was nothing more she could do but be there for her.

While she was in the parlour she heard a knock, so opened the door to find Mr Stenhouse standing there. "I have just heard what happened to Mr Fletcher. How is Miss Emmeline, was she hurt?" he enquired. Jane explained what had happened and that Miss Emmeline was heartbroken and wasn't seeing any visitors. "I am so sorry, please give her my condolences. If I can help in any way, please let me know." That was our Mr Stenhouse, so upper-class English, but she did detect a tiny bit of feeling in his voice. Her mind went back to the night he had consumed too many whiskies and they had to put him to bed.

Another day had passed and Emmeline was still not seeing anyone. Ewan's funeral had been arranged by his mother and because he loved the Lakes District and his current employment, she wanted him to be buried on the hill. He would be with Emmeline's papa ... and his papa! When Emmeline heard where he was to be buried she perked up a little, as she would be able to visit him, and each time she looked up the hill she would be reminded of her beloved Ewan. She hadn't met his family, but tomorrow at the burial she would.

Today was a sad day and Emmeline had closed the collieries for the day so the men could attend Ewan's burial. He was liked and respected by everyone. The miners knew he was trying to get a bill passed in Parliament so collieries would be properly protected by safety regulations. Emmeline, Desmond, Jane, Mr Stenhouse and the groundsman all waited together to join the procession as it started on its journey. Ewan's family led the mourners, walking behind the funeral carriage as it wound its way up the hill. Emmeline was a quivering mess and had to be helped by Jane and Desmond as they followed the procession. She could not believe her beloved Ewan had gone; what would she do now?

It was a cooler day and the lake looked grey and uninviting, it was as if were mourning one of its residents. It had set the mood for the day. Emmeline couldn't remember much about the service, only that when Ewan's coffin was being lowered into the grave, she walked up and fell to her knees and cried for her beloved. She remembered being lifted up and cuddled by a strange lady; this was Ewan's mother. This was the first time they had met, both mourning the loss of a loved one. Emmeline clung to her and told her Ewan was her whole life, that they loved each other dearly. Ewan's mother was a comforting lady and asked her to come and meet his half-siblings. She introduced her as Miss Christian, Ewan's lady friend. They all hugged her, no words were spoken as they were too heartbroken. Emmeline's miners all lined up and shook her hand and bowed their heads in silence. Everyone started to make their way down the hill, but Emmeline wanted time on her own with Ewan. Mr

Stenhouse came up to her and held her hand, then he did the unthinkable: he took her in his arms and held her, and stood and shed tears with her. The tears weren't for Mr Fletcher, they were for Miss Emmeline; to see her so distraught tore at his heart. He stood there with her in his arms until Desmond came and asked him to come with him and to leave Emmeline on her own to mourn.

Jane had studied Ewan's mother as she stood by his grave, but her face didn't seem to fit with the image she had in her head of the lady that came that day with the little boy to Mr Christian's office. Perhaps because it was over fifteen years ago, her memory may have faded. Jane watched her, and she paused at Mr Christian's tombstone; why would she do that? Nothing changed her thoughts on the matter that Ewan was definitely Mr Christian's illegitimate son and to think they were buried side by side on the hill ... how ironic! Would she ever tell Miss Emmeline? Perhaps one day.

Today it was back to the coal-pit for Emmeline as she had a business to run. The collieries still had to be managed, although they had lost their appeal. She wondered if perhaps she should lease them out, then she thought of her uncles. The police were working out how to deal with Ewan's death. The two men knew they would spend years behind bars, so if they implicated the uncles, maybe their sentences would be reduced. It was not meant to be a murder, just a rough-up, but they had botched it up. For Emmeline to be there and recognise them was the worst scenario. When the uncles found out what had happened they were angry, as they had paid the men to frighten Ewan, not murder him, so they were two very worried men.

The next month went by and Emmeline was still in

mourning; she spent more of her time down by the lake. She looked across at Belle isle and thought of Isabella. This was not how her life was meant to work out, but now she was left in the same position as her heroine. There were two cousins, not her cousins, but nevertheless they were cousins. Was this her future? She could not think clearly, she was living in her own little world; there were only two people in it, her and Ewan. She was reliving their intimate times together. He was a noble young man, not wishing to take what was offered to him, but instead lived by his principles. She would never find a love this deep, ever!

As time went by the pain became less. Emmeline had immersed herself in work, and the miners all loved her. They felt her pain. Now that the second 'nark' was gone, the collieries were a safe place once more. She spent more time with Desmond and his son, they were her rocks. They would take the cart to the farmlet often, so little John could play with the animals and the children. They had two new calves, the piglets were no more, as they had grown into greedy pigs. The families were kept in eggs and milk. Soon Emmeline would borrow a ram to put with the sheep so they could get lambs, then they would have a supply of meat, something they could very rarely afford to buy.

Desmond felt close to Emmeline but he did not make any advances towards her. Having been in the same position, he knew it took a long time to feel deeply for another person. She was still in mourning. Little John had high hopes that one day she would be his new mummy, as he loved her and she loved him. Mr Stenhouse watched as Miss Emmeline became part of their lives again. It had been painful watching her suffer, as his heart had suffered alongside hers.

While down at the lake, Emmeline spent many hours trying to work out if in the end her path was taking the same as her heroine. The two cousins — was this the sign? If her life was going to follow Isabella's then she would love Desmond and his son and Mr Stenhouse would be the one that loved her most, but he wasn't the chosen one. Was Ewan only lent to her for a short time to teach her about love? She could see herself loving Desmond one day, but Mr Stenhouse, definitely not! She had to admit he had changed his ways. He was not so stuffy any more and he actually laughed, which made him look more his age, and the twitches seem to have disappeared, thank goodness. Perhaps this was because he said he loved someone. One day she would ask him, but now wasn't the time, she didn't want to talk about love.

The men who murdered Ewan were sent to jail but the uncles were never mentioned. Emmeline didn't think this was fair as they were the ones that had paid the men. She heard they were going to reopen their colliery, and she was heartbroken and angry; because of them she didn't have her Ewan. She wanted them punished. She went to her papa's desk and took out the letter about the ownership of the collieries, and read through it several times. It said it was a verbal gift of land and colliery to his brothers; if it was not recorded legally on paper then could she demand it all back? She would ask Mr Stenhouse how they stood on this matter. She went straight to his office and asked if she could see him. He always made time for Miss Emmeline, he couldn't see her often enough. "Come in, how can I help you?" he asked politely. "Could you please read through these papers and tell me if my uncles legally own the land and colliery, or does it still belong to Papa? Is a verbal gift legally binding?" "Miss Emmeline, you are becoming a sharp young lady. No, a verbal gift is not a binding document. This was your father helping out his brothers, but he still owned the land and the colliery, it is in his name. And now that he is deceased, his estate is yours." "Does that mean I can take it from them?" she asked. "Why do that? Why not let them run it but demand royalties? Make it tough for them. Miss Emmeline, while you are here we must discuss your wealth. You are very wealthy; is there anything you would like to do with your money? Your father did mention you dreamt about buying an island in Lake Windermere. Is this what you would like to do?" "I have always dreamed of my own island but I don't know if I can afford it," she said. "You have enough money to buy two islands and build two mansions, Miss Emmeline, you have no idea of your wealth. If that is what you want to do, do it!" Mr Stenhouse thought this was a wonderful idea as it would give her a standing in society where she belonged. She would be up there with the upper class; to own an island with a mansion, only the really wealthy were afforded this luxury. One only had to look across to Belle Isle and remember Isabella Curwen and her wealth; it was still talked about. Miss Emmeline was no different, but he did remember they were related.

Emmeline had one nagging thought in her head: Thomas had to be found as he was entitled to half her fortune. Only she and Jane even knew he existed; perhaps she would discuss it again with Jane. "I will draw up a written lease for you to present to your uncles, we will surprise them. We will hold a meeting here in my office; it will be very interesting to see how they feel being hassled." Emmeline hated the thought of being in the same room as her uncles, but now she could make their lives miserable, just as they had done to her. She thanked Mr Stenhouse and as she went to the door he went with her and put his hand on her shoulder. "Are you managing okay? Please let me help you if I can; you helped me realise my stuffiness to which I am changing. I care deeply for you, Miss Emmeline." She smiled at him through tear-filled eyes, as any mention of what had happened was still raw. "That is nice of you, Edward. Could you please look into how I can purchase my island?" He agreed to get on to it straight away, anything to lift her position on the society ladder. His friend George and other friends had requested that he bring Emmeline to one of their social nights again, as they had enjoyed her company when they met for drinks. He couldn't do it any time soon; the timing wasn't right.

As she made her way home she decided to call on Desmond and little John. She would discuss with them about her dream of an 'Emerald Isle' and see what they thought. They were both happy to see her and little John ran to her for his motherly cuddle. She sat down and told them what she wanted to do. They thought it was a wonderful idea. "I want you both to draw a picture of what you think I should build on the island." This Desmond would be good at, as he loved to draw. Their friendship was close although it had never progressed beyond being friends, because he could see Emmeline was still hurting. They felt comfortable with each other and this was enough to hold them together for the moment.

Several weeks later Mr Stenhouse called into Miss Emmeline's on his way home after work. He had some news for her, so she asked him to come through to her papa's office. They sat down and he produced a leaflet on an island called Thompson's Holme, which was situated northwest of Belle Isle and had a little beach on the southern end. It was not nearly as large as Belle Isle but it was the largest of all the other islands. If she wanted to have a look he would arrange a trip across the lake for them. Emmeline was excited. Was this the beginning of her dream come true? Was she going to have her own isle? Her neighbouring island would be Belle Isle. Yes, she asked Mr Stenhouse to arrange a trip across the lake as soon as possible. He also had other business to discuss with her. He had arranged a meeting at his office with her uncles for the following day. He didn't disclose to them what the meeting was about — let them think perhaps they were going to get Miss Emmeline's collieries to lease. But whatever their thinking, they were in for a big shock.

Emmeline arrived at Mr Stenhouse's office a few minutes before her uncles were due. She was nervous and upset as she had not seen them since before Ewan's death. When they came into the office they were shocked to see Emmeline sitting there. They looked at each other not daring to look at her, so didn't acknowledge Emmeline. "The reason we are here today, gentlemen, is because Emmeline has a proposition to put to you. I don't know if you are aware that she owns your land and your colliery," he stated. "But that is not right, it is ours, our brother gave it to us," they said in anger. "Yes, your brother verbally gifted it to you but nothing was recorded or signed; the deeds are still in Mr Christian's name. Now that he is deceased his estate passed on to his daughter; she is the sole beneficiary therefore owns your land and colliery. We believe you are going to reopen the colliery, is this correct?" "Yes, we are doing that at this very moment," they answered. "Right, Miss Emmeline, put your proposal forward," announced Mr Stenhouse. "I own the land and the colliery, therefore you will pay me royalties. If this is not suitable to you then you can move off my land. You have caused me such pain, now I am going to teach you what pain really is. The royalties will be the price you offered me for the lease of my collieries." "But that was a high payment, we will struggle to make a living," they replied angrily. "The choice is yours; pay the royalties or move off the land," they were told in no uncertain terms. The uncles were shafted, just the position she wanted them in. They looked at her with disgust; fancy working for their niece and feeding her coffers. Mr Stenhouse said he would draw up a contract for them to sign if they wanted the colliery. They really had no choice! They stood up and without a word to Emmeline they left the office.

16

Was Emmeline's Dream about to Happen?

Today Emmeline and Mr Stenhouse were on the boat on their way to Thompson's Holme island. To be standing and watching the enchanted Belle Isle in the distance, she felt the excitement start to well up in her body, a feeling she hadn't had for a long time. As they came closer to Thompson's Holme, Emmeline's excitement grew and before she realised she was hugging Mr Stenhouse with such enthusiasm she nearly knocked him over. Not that he would complain; he loved every moment she made bodily contact with him. Where the island was Emmeline's wildest dream, she was Mr Stenhouse's absolute dream, so this visit was going to bring a range of feelings, if for different reasons. They pulled up in the boat at the southern end of the island and made arrangements with the boat owner to pick them up in two hours. Emmeline took Mr Stenhouse's hand and helped him up onto the bank. This was a bit back-to-front, he thought, it should have been him helping her to alight. He would have to think quicker next time! They walked until they had a clear view of the vistas surrounding the island. Emmeline's heart melted, she was frozen in time; in front of her lay her dream: her Emerald Isle, Isabella's enchanted Belle Isle, and in the far distance she could make out the outline of the hill where her Ewan and her papa lay at rest. This was her serene peace.

She sat down and closed her eyes; she felt the warmth of the earth, she breathed in the fresh air, and her feelings ran wild. The only other place that held this feeling was Ewan's cottage by the lake. Mr Stenhouse watched this beautiful creature who was lost in a world of her own. She suddenly stood up and twirled around and around with her arms outstretched; how he wished he was part of her magical dream. He had never been in this situation before, and never seen such an outward display of joy. There was no excitement like this in his stuffy narrow life, and yet here it was, right in front of him. He wanted to be part of it; could he break down his barrier and act semi-normal, did he have the guts to act abnormal?

"Come, Edward, take your shoes off and feel the magic of this place, be part of it with me," she pleaded. How could he refuse? This was the time and place to prove he was at least a tiny bit human. He knelt down, untied his shoelaces, and slipped off his shoes and socks, putting them in a neat pile. How very Mr Stenhouse, she thought. Then she had the urge to run up and kick the neat pile apart, and this she did. He stood and watched in disbelief; why did she do that? Emmeline came to him and took his hand and encouraged him to run with her along the lake front. He had never acted in this way before; what was happening to him? All his inhibitions flew out the window; here was a grown man doing silly things, but strangely enough he was enjoying himself. He had never felt this happiness ever, even when he was a child he didn't show such childish behaviour. "I will race you back," Emmeline yelled as she let go of his hand, then she took off. Edward found an inner strength and a will to prove to her that he could indeed run, so halfway down the island he overtook her. She was amazed, but had to stop and laugh, as here was a man dressed in a suit and barefooted racing her. He came back and wanted to know what was so funny and when she explained, he actually did see the funny side. "Edward, this new love you have found has made you a different man. You must tell me about her one day." "I promise you I will, but I need a little more time. You are a bad influence on me, Miss Emmeline, I have never acted so silly even when I was a child, but thank you, I have had a wonderful day." He sat down and put his shoes and socks on and became Mr Stenhouse once again.

Their trip back on the boat was spent in silence, both thinking about the island but for different reasons. But in a mixed-up way they both felt love; one for an island, the other for another. Emmeline asked Mr Stenhouse to purchase the island on her behalf and she would sign the papers. He was happy for her to make this purchase, as he could see her climbing the social ladder. Perhaps one day they could both run barefooted around the island again, but next time he would catch her and take her in his arms and love her.

Another year had passed and the building of the mansion was well under way. Desmond had drawn up a plan that Emmeline loved, so it was given to a draughtsman to finalise. They spent many Saturdays at Emerald Isle checking to see that all was progressing favourably. Mr Stenhouse was feeling rather neglected as it was Desmond that was Miss Emmeline's constant companion ... not him! His friends, especially George, had asked him many times to bring Emmeline back to one of their social gatherings, so he hoped to find the courage to ask her next time she was at his office. The uncles were in business again with their colliery, but to have to pay their niece a royalty really hit a nerve with them. They had heard she had bought an island on Lake Windermere and was building a mansion; this made the pain more unbearable, as she was growing wealthier and they were helping her cause. But there was no alternative. They had messed with her life once and it went horribly wrong; they couldn't afford a second shot. At least with the colliery they could make themselves a moderate living.

The school year was drawing to an end for the children that Emmeline had supported. Desmond had watched these children progressing into individuals who loved the privilege of attending classes. He was going to approach Emmeline to see if she would extend their education for another year, to get a better picture of how well they were doing and if indeed they were prepared to stick with it to make better lives for themselves. He felt one year wasn't enough to get an overall assessment. Desmond and little

John called in at Emmeline's home and were met at the door by Jane. She really liked him and his son and encouraged them all she could, hoping he and Miss Emmeline would form a relationship. She showed them through to the drawing room where Emmeline was curled up in her chair reading a book. She jumped up and greeted them with a hug. "Miss Emmeline, at last I have remembered to bring you the photo of Granny and me, it has been in my drawer all this time. It was taken when I was a baby, but look at me now, I've grown big but my granny is the same," he said proudly. Emmeline laughed and took the photo and commented on how he had certainly grown. She had forgotten she had asked him to bring back a photo while he was holidaying with his granny. Gosh, that was over a year ago. She put the photo on the mantelpiece above the fireplace. Desmond seized this moment to ask Emmeline if she would consider giving the children she supported at school another year to see how they progressed. "Of course, Desmond, they deserve the chance to be educated. If they want to continue, let them have the opportunity, I want to help them." "That is kind of you, Emmeline. Tomorrow I can send them home with a letter telling their mothers they can come back to school for another year." They chatted for a while then made arrangements for another trip out to the island the next Sunday.

On Monday she called in to Mr Stenhouse's office to see if her uncles' contract had been signed and was all legal, of which it was; they had accepted all her terms. "Miss Emmeline, my friends have asked me to bring you along to our social gathering on Friday night. Will you accompany me? I promise to be on my best behaviour this time," he said sheepishly. "That will be nice, I will be able to tell them about the children they gave donations to." He was very happy that she accepted, because he would take her away from Desmond. He was becoming increasingly jealous of his cousin; he was a mere schoolteacher, where he himself was a solicitor. This was the difference between being working class as opposed to upper class.

Later on in the week while Emmeline was in her office at the coal-pit, a strange carriage pulled up in front of the building and out stepped two official-looking men. They came to the office and asked for a Mr Ewan Fletcher. Poor Emmeline; as soon as Ewan's name was mentioned her eyes filled with tears. She told them he was not here any more, so they wanted to know where they could contact him. She could not answer them as her trickle of tears had turned into streams. One of the office men came to her rescue and introduced her as Miss Christian, their employer. When he told them what had happened to Ewan, they were upset. "We came to tell Mr Fletcher his bill is being passed in Parliament and to present him with an award. We are deeply sorry for what has happened; he was a very passionate man towards the safety of the miners, and his thesis covered all the loopholes in the safety aspects of the collieries. Would you like to accept this award on his behalf?" they asked Emmeline. She wiped away her tears and thanked them very much. "Ewan would have been proud to hear he was listened to and that his bill was being passed; he cared deeply for the miners. I will visit him and let him know," she told the men. They congratulated her on her commitment to safety at her collieries, as Ewan had mentioned that Miss Christian's collieries were the best example of any he had seen. With this they shook her hand and took their leave. Emmeline told her staff she would take the award up to Ewan straight away to let him know his greatest wish had been granted, his bill was going to be passed through Parliament. She wanted to share this moment with him. She drove the carriage to the bottom of the hill and walked up as she had done so many times before to where he lay in peace. She knelt by his grave and expressed all her feelings and outbursts with him, then as she was leaving, she sealed her visit with a kiss on his headstone. He was her greatest love ever ... would this change? She took the award back to the coal-pit and hung it in the entrance way so the miners would remember the man that went to battle for them.

Mr Stenhouse's carriage pulled up at the entrance to Miss Emmeline's home. He sat and reflected for a moment. He had gone to his friend George for advice on what to wear, so George took him shopping to buy less formal clothes. He actually felt quite proud of how he looked. He almost could not recognise himself as he stood in front of the mirror; he had to wave just to make sure the image waved back. He hoped Miss Emmeline would like his new look and himself as well. He knocked at the door and Jane opened it. "Wow, is that you, Mr Stenhouse?" she asked. She took him through to the drawing room. When Emmeline saw him she could not believe what her eyes were showing her. "Why, Edward, you look so different. I certainly couldn't call you Mr Stenhouse tonight, because you look nothing like him. Who is this new man?" Edward felt very proud that his Miss Emmeline obviously liked his new look. Could she be persuaded to love him? "You look lovely tonight, Miss Emmeline, but then you always do ... to me," he added. She told him to drop the formalities for tonight as they were going out as friends.

They walked to the carriage and he offered for her to sit inside but she wanted to ride up front with him. As he helped her up he made sure his hand didn't brush her bottom ... not like last time! As they drove off to Ambleside, Emmeline told Edward about the two official men who had brought an award to present to Ewan, as his bill was being passed through Parliament. She could hardly get it all out, as she was choked with tears. This was not what he wanted to hear, not that name, but he knew sympathy would be appropriate in this situation. "I'm so sorry, Emmeline, he was a good man." He reached over and took her hand, and she moved closer to him, so he put his arm around her. This was how they travelled the rest of the way. Emmeline was feeling comforted, while Edward's love was flourishing.

When they arrived at the inn, she put her sad memories behind her so she could enjoy the night. Edward helped her down and tied the horses to the hitching rails. They walked in together, but this time he didn't have to rush off to the men's room and leave Emmeline on her own. His confidence had grown, the twitches were gone, forever he hoped, and now she seemed to have a calming effect on him. George was the first person to see them. He came up and took Emmeline's arm and led her off, instructing Edward to bring the drinks. "What do you think of the new look Edward?" he asked her. She told him she was totally surprised. "You know, Emmeline, he is sweet on you." With this she told George that he had met someone he loved, so she was happy for him. The conversation stopped dead in its tracks. Edward came over with a wine for Emmeline and a whisky for himself and for George, and they went to meet the rest of the party. They were all pleased to see her again. Someone asked how the miners' children were, and she was able to say she had extended their education for another year to give them a chance to excel and thanked them for their support, as their money went into school books for the children. They all clapped.

During the evening she met a lady who owned a haberdashery shop in Ambleside. As they talked and got to know each other, she invited Emmeline to visit her shop next time she was in town. She stocked all items of clothing and now knowing of Emmeline's wealth, she could certainly show her beautiful things. Edward had told George who Emmeline was and that she was one of the wealthiest young ladies in all of Cumbria. This information had filtered pretty quickly through the group, so everyone wanted to be her friend. And to find out she had bought an island in Lake Windermere and was building a mansion on the island had to be the best bit of gossip. Edward was the envy of all his friends, as they had just presumed they were an item ... or had he told them so? He stuck close to her and seized every moment that was available to put his arm around her. She was rather enjoying herself tonight. She was on her second glass of wine and her head felt relieved of all tension and past thoughts; even Edward looked like any young man that would attract her attention. He seemed very affectionate tonight.

The party all moved to the dining room to have dinner. A large table had been arranged for them, so they could all dine together. Emmeline had Edward on one side and George on the other; she noticed he was on his own tonight. They ordered their food, had a few toasts and talked nonstop until they were ready to eat. Then George stood up and asked everyone to raise their glasses to toast Edward and Emmeline. What for? everyone wanted to know. "To a new friendship," he stated. She thought this was rather funny, as she and Edward were already friends as such. Edward was most embarrassed and asked George to sit down. No one knew the true relationship between them.

Emmeline paid particular notice to Edward's eating habits and yes, they had changed; he now ate like a normal person. She asked Edward to fill her glass again as it was empty. "Are you sure, Emmeline? This will be your third." "Oh Edward, don't be so stuffy, I'm nearly nineteen, I'm not a child," she scolded him. As he left the table she felt a hand on her knee, and realised it belonged to George. "I'm not available, George, not at the moment," she whispered. With this he promptly withdrew his hand. Edward came back with a half glass of wine, as he felt responsible for her and didn't want her to be ill the next day.

The night was enjoyed by all and farewells were expressed in hugs all round. George's hug was more a crush than a hug; he was one to watch out for!

Edward went to fetch the carriage and Emmeline insisted on sitting up front with him to get some fresh air. It was no easy task to help her up as she was a little wobbly, but he managed, always aware not to touch her inappropriately. As he climbed up he was a little concerned for Emmeline as she was having trouble sitting up straight. "Emmeline, I think you would be better in the carriage, I think you will be safer in there." "Don't worry, Edward, I have you to hold on to, I don't bite," she told him. With that she put her arms firmly around his waist. As they were going along the road, her hair was brushing against his face and he could smell her perfume. Oh Emmeline, if only you were mine, he thought to himself. Emmeline closed her eyes; her head was fuzzy and all she could think about was Ewan, he was here with her. She reached up and pulled his head down and kissed him on the lips. She moved her arms from around his waist and put them around his neck encouraging him to respond to her. This startled Edward; he was beside himself. What should he do? Was it the wine taking hold? Did she know what she was doing? Would he be taking advantage of her? He decided to gently return her kiss, and this was all the encouragement she needed. She started kissing him passionately, then tried to undo his shirt buttons so she could touch his bare skin. Edward was stunned; this didn't happen until two people were married, only then did they have the right to touch each other's bare flesh. He pulled on the reins for the horses to stop. They stopped quickly and Emmeline's dream came to a sudden end. "What happened, is something wrong?" she asked. Then reality took over; she realised what she had done and burst into tears. "I'm so sorry, Edward, please forgive me. I don't know what came over me." But all the time she did, but she couldn't tell him she thought he was Ewan. "Don't cry, Emmeline, you have had too much to drink, you weren't in control of yourself," he said, trying to comfort her.

Back at Emmeline's stately home Jane had decided to do her housework while waiting for Miss Emmeline to return home. She went into the drawing room and started her dusting. As she dusted the mantelpiece, something fell on the floor so she bent down to pick it up and put it back. She noticed it was a photo. That's strange, she thought, she had never noticed it before, so she turned it over to see if she knew who it was. It was a photo of a lady and a little boy. As soon as she saw the lady her memory came flooding back. That was the lady that came to Mr Christian's home with the little boy all those years ago. She remembered him taking them into his office and shutting the door, then when they came out he walked to the front entrance and called 'Goodbye, Thomas.' How did it get here? Who did it belong to? She studied the photo again but couldn't make out who the child was. But that was the lady, no mistaking. No wonder she didn't recognise Ewan's mother, she was nothing like this lady. So, she was wrong, Ewan was not Mr Christian's illegitimate son; then who was? Jane felt sick; imagine if she had told Miss Emmeline what she had presumed. She tried to think if the photo was there last time she dusted; if it was she would have seen it. No, it must have been put there recently. Why hadn't Miss Emmeline shown it to her? She couldn't wait for her to arrive home, then she would ask her about the photo.

17

The Unspeakable Truth

As Edward pulled up at the front entrance he looked at Emmeline and her tears were still falling. He let go of the reins and took her in his arms. "It's all right, Emmeline, don't be sad, this will never be discussed again. You weren't in control, it is as if it never happened." But this was of small comfort to her. What was wrong with him, did he not enjoy her advances? Perhaps it was because he loved someone else. She had just lost her way tonight. Never did she think of Edward as anyone but a friend. Was her behaviour tonight because Ewan's memory had been revived this week? She still missed him so much. Edward helped her down and brushed away her tears. "Go to bed,

Emmeline, you will feel better tomorrow." He walked her to the door and thanked her for a lovely night.

Emmeline went inside and burst into tears. Jane heard her come home and came out to meet her. When she saw Miss Emmeline crying she put her arms around her to comfort her not knowing what had happened. "I made a fool of myself with Edward tonight," she said. She explained how she thought for one moment he was Ewan. Poor Miss Emmeline, she was still fretting for her lost love, but she had another pressing matter to attend to. "Miss Emmeline, while I was dusting the mantelpiece in the drawing room, a photo fell on the floor. I have never seen it before; how long has it been there?" "It is new; little John gave it to me," she said. "Who is the photo of?" asked Jane. "That is little John's granny. It is Desmond's mother." With this explanation Jane could not believe what she had just heard, if fact she didn't want to believe it; this was turning into a nightmare. She couldn't get her head around it; that meant Desmond was Mr Christian's illegitimate son, therefore Miss Emmeline and Desmond were half-siblings. To think she had encouraged this friendship, oh my God, what was going to happen? Just how far had the friendship developed? "Are you all right, Jane? You look terrible," she said. "No, I'm not well, I will go to bed," said Jane as she made her way up the stairs. She could not face Miss Emmeline for another moment; she felt sick. Who could she go to, who could she discuss this with? She had to talk to someone ... but who? The only person that knew the family business was of course Mr Stenhouse, but weren't he and Desmond cousins? Jane didn't want this to go outside of the family so it would have to be discussed with Mr Stenhouse. Emmeline went to bed and slept the night away, while Jane lay awake all night, upset with what had transpired today. She would never have believed this in her wildest dreams; now she was faced with a nightmare. Tomorrow was Saturday, but she would have to go to Mr Stenhouse's home as she couldn't wait until Monday. How was she going to face Miss Emmeline in the morning? She would take leave for the day until she knew how to handle this dire situation.

The next morning when Emmeline arose, she remembered last night all too well and her actions towards Edward. She was so embarrassed. While with him on a social scale as Edward it didn't seem quite so bad, but on a day-to-day basis as Mr Stenhouse she was shocked; what did he really think of her? He had two different personalities. By the time she dressed and went downstairs to the parlour it was mid-morning. Where was Jane? Then she saw a note on the bench: Jane had gone out early and wouldn't be back until later. This was indeed unusual for her, but then she remembered that she wasn't well last night. Emmeline hoped she was all right.

Jane had walked around to Mr Stenhouse's in the hope he was at home. She knocked on his door and waited. When he saw Jane standing there he immediately thought something was wrong with Miss Emmeline. "Please, may I come in, Mr Stenhouse? I have to talk to someone; I don't know what to do," she pleaded. "Calm down, Jane, what has happened?" She didn't know where to start; it was so complicated so she just sat in silence. Then she broke down. "I have had such a shock," she said between her tears and she struggled to get any more words out. Where would she start? "Did you know Mr Christian had an illegitimate son?" "No, I didn't, are you sure?" he asked. "Yes, it is true. When Mr Christian was dying he asked Miss Emmeline to find 'Thomas'. I have just found him but

Miss Emmeline doesn't know. How can I tell her?" "If it is going to change things, does she have to know? We don't have to tell her if it is going to upset her. This would mean he would be entitled to half her wealth," said a concerned Mr Stenhouse. "But I have to tell her, and she will be heartbroken again. I don't want to do it, but she must know," sobbed Jane. Mr Stenhouse was wondering why all the fuss and why was Jane so upset? "It is Desmond. Desmond is Mr Christian's illegitimate son." "What do you mean? He can't be, no, it's not true, he is my cousin, I would have known," he stammered. "It is true. I saw the photo little John gave to Miss Emmeline, it was of him and his grandmother, and as soon as I saw it I recognised the lady. She was the same lady that came to Mr Christian's home with a little boy about sixteen years ago and he called him 'Thomas'. That is why we have to tell them — they can't be in a relationship as they are half-siblings."

If Jane hadn't qualified that this was true, he would never have believed it. As he thought about it, it worked two ways for him. It took Desmond out of the equation as far as Miss Emmeline was concerned, but far more stinging he was now a very wealthy young man and was entitled to half Miss Emmeline's fortune. Even the collieries would be half owned by him. Desmond, he couldn't take this in, Mr Christian's illegitimate son, how did he not know, why hadn't his family told him? He was stunned by this news, and offered to make Jane a cup of tea while they both tried to work out what to do. "I can't face Miss Emmeline knowing this, as I encouraged this relationship. I am worried as I don't know how far it has developed," said a worried Jane. Suddenly Mr Stenhouse thought back to Miss Emmeline's behaviour last night, and he went cold. If she acted the same with Desmond, would he have taken advantage of her, as he was younger? They both sat and stared at each other, neither knowing where to start. "What do we do, Mr Stenhouse?" asked Jane as she broke the silence. This was the first time in his life that something had such a profound impact, one that left him stunned and, like Jane, not knowing what to do or where to start. Who would tell who, was the biggest problem at the moment. "Do you think you could tell Miss Emmeline, and once she knows she might be able to break it to Desmond?" asked Mr Stenhouse. Jane said she would try to find the right moment to tell her, but she couldn't promise anything. They left it at that and she would report back to him.

Jane left Mr Stenhouse's in the same black mood that she arrived with, as nothing had been solved. It looked as if it was up to her to break this devastating news to Miss Emmeline. She could not go back to the home; she needed to clear her head so she walked along the lake to Miss Emmeline's favourite place, where she sat down to think. As she was sitting there she saw Desmond and little John walking towards her. "Hello, Miss Jane!" yelled little John. They came up and sat down to talk to her. "We are going to Emerald Isle with Miss Emmeline tomorrow to see how the builders are going," he told her. She asked Desmond if he had any brothers or sisters, but he said he was an only child and he lived with his mother and grandparents. He didn't know anything about his father as he was never discussed. This was definitely Mr Christian's son, thought Jane. She had to ask Desmond something: "How is everything going between you and Miss Emmeline?" "I like her very much, we are very close friends. Once she gets over losing Ewan things will be a lot easier; it takes a long time to recover from a lost love," he said. Then little John became part of the conversation. "I want Miss Emmeline to be my new mummy one day. She loves me and I love her." This broke Jane's heart to hear this from this little boy, he had so much hope for the future ... one that could never be! "I saw the photo of little John with his granny; she is a fine-looking lady. Where does she live?" asked Jane. "My mother lives in Whitehaven. She inherited her parents' home when they passed on. It is a lovely home, isn't it, son?" "Yes, I love Granny Bridget's home." Out of this conversation came the name of Desmond's mother ... Bridget Stenhouse.

The next morning Jane left early to catch the train to Whitehaven. She had left a picnic basket for Miss Emmeline to take to the island. When she arrived in Whitehaven she enquired at the railway store to see if anyone knew of Bridget Stenhouse. The lady behind the counter asked around and found out her address. She would have to take a carriage as the home was on the outskirts of town. She arranged a carriage for Jane.

When they pulled up outside the large home she asked the driver to wait for a moment until she could see if anyone was at home. She knocked on the door and it was opened by the lady that was in the photo. Jane asked if she could come in and talk to her. She then went back to the carriage driver and asked him to come back within the hour. Jane walked back to the door and introduced herself. The lady asked her to come in and said she was Bridget Stenhouse, how could she help her? Jane started the conversation by saying that she had seen a photo of her with her grandson John. "Oh, so you know Desmond and John?" she asked. "Yes, I work for Miss Emmeline Christian as her housekeeper." As soon as Jane mentioned the name Christian, the lady sat upright. "I have worked in the Christian household for many years and when I saw you in the photo, I recognised you from about sixteen years ago when you came with your little boy to Mr Christian's home. His name was 'Thomas'. Did you know that Desmond and Miss Emmeline are in a relationship?" "Oh no, that can't happen. That can't be true, please tell me that's not true," she pleaded. "That is why I am here today, I had to find out for sure you were that lady."

Bridget Stenhouse broke down and told Jane that they would be half-siblings. She said she hadn't told anyone who Desmond's father was as she didn't want to cause a scandal. "I don't know how to handle this," said Jane. "Emmeline is going to have her heart broken again, I'm frightened it will be too much for her. This is going to change their lives forever and with it will come more heartache." Bridget Stenhouse never in a hundred years would have suspected her past was going to come back and haunt her, and ruin two other lives along the way. She told Jane she would catch the train to Bowness the next day and break this devastating news to her son, as no one else could do it, it was her responsibility. Jane said she would try to break the news to Miss Emmeline within the next couple of days. Bridget Stenhouse thanked Jane for coming and being discreet about the situation. With that, Jane took her leave as the carriage was waiting for her to take her back to the train station.

Emmeline, Desmond and little John had a great day on Emerald Isle. They had their picnic and watched the builders working on the roof. The mansion was shaping up nicely; another nine months should see it finished. It was a Tudor-style home with lattice windows. Desmond had designed the front porch with the round pillars like on Belle Isle to remember that eventful day they rowed out to the island. He remembered dancing through the trees with Emmeline in his arms, then the three of them huddled together on the porch waiting for the wind to abate and the waves to lessen. This was a lasting memory, as he knew that day he had feelings for Emmeline. She was a dreamer and a free spirit just like him. They were similar in many ways and now that the truth was going to be revealed ... it all made sense. Of course they were similar, they were half-siblings! This would be devastating news to one little person in particular, one who wanted Miss Emmeline to be his new mummy, but far worse for his father.

When Emmeline arrived home, Jane was still not there. She was concerned; where would she have gone for the day? This had happened twice this week, was something wrong? She set about to make a sandwich for tea when she heard the door shut and into the parlour came Jane. "Is something wrong, Jane, are you not well?" she asked. "I have been feeling unwell but I will come right," she answered. "We had a lovely day on the island, we walked all over it and made plans for the gardens and where to plant our trees; it was as if we were a family." The word family was too much for Jane to bear; she left the parlour and ran upstairs to her bedroom and shut the door. How was she going to tell Miss Emmeline when they were planning their future? She lay there wishing it would go away but with each day it became worse. Desmond's mother was arriving the next day, so he would know then or the day after. She would have to tell her tomorrow.

She heard a knock on her door. "Jane, I have made you a sandwich, can I come in please?" "Just a moment." With this she tidied herself and went to the door. "Let me sit with you. Something is wrong, you have been avoiding me. Please tell me what it is." With this she put her arms around Miss Emmeline and the tears flowed. Now was the time! "You remember your papa telling you before he passed away to find 'Thomas'? I have found him — he is your half-brother. Mr Christian was his father as well as yours." "So, I have a sibling, that is great news. When can I meet him?" she asked. "You have already met him, Miss Emmeline. Desmond is your half-brother." On hearing this she let out a piercing scream. "No, Jane, no, tell me that's not true," she sobbed. "I'm sorry, Miss Emmeline, but it is true. I went to Whitehaven today and met Desmond's mother, Bridget Stenhouse, and she confirmed it. When I saw the photo of little John and his granny, I knew then it was the same lady that came all those years ago. She had no idea that Desmond even knew you until I told her that you were very good friends. She is coming down on the train tomorrow to speak with Desmond. We knew you both had to learn the truth as soon as possible." "But we are more than just friends, Jane, what are we going to do?" Jane held her tight and they cried together; this was devastating news.

Now she had lost her second love, but it was not such a profound loss as her first love. This one was only just starting, and now it had to end. What was happening? This wasn't how she had planned her life. All those years of dreaming were wasted, she was shattered. Her life was meant to be straightforward as was Isabella's, but something had gone horribly wrong. Now she was left with only the one cousin, Mr Stenhouse. Was he her future? She didn't want to think that far ahead. She had to come to terms with losing Desmond.

She thanked Jane for telling her the truth, now she just wanted time on her own. She couldn't go down by the lake for fear of meeting Desmond, so she decided to climb the hill and sit with her papa and let him know she had found 'Thomas'. As complicated as it was, he would have been happy they had found each other. As this news slowly sunk into Emmeline's head, she could see the likeness between her and Desmond. At their very first meeting they admitted they were dreamers and free spirits. They both cared about the miners' children who were without schooling and their values were similar, something that had obviously been passed down through their father's genes. Although they could never be lovers because they were connected through blood, they could continue to be good friends, and their plans for Emerald Isle could still go ahead as now Desmond would be a part owner. This truth would change their lives forever; new paths would have to be taken.

The next day, Bridget Stenhouse arrived at her son's home. Little John was over the moon to see his granny. He told her about yesterday at the island where Daddy and Miss Emmeline were going to plant their trees and put their gardens. "You should see it, Granny, Miss Emmeline owns the island and one day Daddy and I will live there with her." Bridget Stenhouse was shaken to the core; this she wished she had never heard. School had just finished for the day, so Desmond was rushing around trying to get his home organised for this unexpected visit by his mother. "I am only staying one night, Desmond, it is a quick visit," she told him. "Please stay longer, Granny, come with us and meet Miss Emmeline, she is going to be my new mummy one day." With this she burst into tears and little John ran to her and cuddled her. "What is wrong, mother?" Desmond asked. "Can we talk alone? I have something I must tell you." Desmond asked his son to play outside for a while as Granny wanted to talk with him.

She told him to sit next to her as she was going to tell him something that was going to hurt him deeply. "Desmond, I never spoken to you about your father, as I thought it best left untold, but you have to know now. I came to Bowness as an eighteen-year-old and met a man and we had an affair. When I found out I was with child, I left and went to live with my parents. When you were seven years old I came back to Bowness with you and we met your father. I told him your name was Thomas. He gave me money for your education, as he was a wealthy man. This was the last contact we had with each other as he had married and had a child. Your father was Mr Christian."

Desmond was shocked. What did this mean, where did it leave him and Emmeline? This meant he was her half-brother, but he loved her! "Mother, I love Emmeline, she makes me happy, we have shared so many things together ..." Then he stopped. He put his head in his hands and once again the heartache returned, the very heartache he had just got over; now he was losing his new love. Bridget Stenhouse didn't know what to say to her son; this was her secret and she thought she was going to take it to her grave. It was a scandal that had been hidden for years, if not for Jane knowing ... but thank God, she did! "I had a visit from Jane, Emmeline's housemaid, as she recognised me from a photo little John had given to Emmeline. She had to be sure she had her facts right. I'm so sorry, Desmond, but imagine if you and Miss Emmeline didn't know, it would have been tragic." "But mother, what is going to happen to us now? Does Emmeline know?" he asked. "Jane was going to tell her as soon as she felt she could, so I don't know."

The damage was done; where to from here? With this, little John came bounding in. "Miss Emmeline is coming, I can see her." Desmond froze, not knowing how he would react. How was this going to affect their relationship? He didn't know how he would handle this, so he left the room. Little John brought Emmeline in to meet his granny. "Granny, this is Miss Emmeline, she loves me," he said in all innocence. Bridget Stenhouse took one look at this lovely young lady standing in front of her and burst into tears. Emmeline guessed that she had told Desmond the truth. She went over to her and reached for her hand as a gesture of friendship. "I'm so sorry for all this pain I have caused," she said to Emmeline. Then Desmond appeared. They stood and looked at each other. The truth had hurt them both but their friendship was deep, it would survive this. Emmeline went to him and took him in her arms knowing he needed comforting, just as she did, and they were the only two that could bring the much-needed comfort to each other. "See, Daddy and Miss Emmeline love each other," said a happy little boy. "Why are you crying, Granny?" he asked. With this he went over to her and hugged her telling her everything would be all right ... if only.

Bridget asked little John to take her for a walk along the lake as she wanted Desmond and Emmeline to have time together. Emmeline asked Desmond to sit down as they had to talk about their feelings. She could see he was devastated, perhaps more so than her, as she was not completely over losing Ewan. But she knew one day she would love Desmond and that time was getting close. "Emmeline, you have brought me such happiness, what happens to us now?" She told him they were close friends and they would carry on being friends, it was just that they couldn't take it any further than a friendship. "We are blood related, no wonder we are so alike. We are brother and sister, we are both dreamers and free spirits, we will get through this, we are family." This is why he loved Emmeline; her dreams carried her through life, she faced challenges head-on. She had faced many challenges in her young life, more so than most. Emmeline felt hurt like everyone else, but she knew hurt healed, it didn't last forever; Desmond had told her this at their first meeting by the lake. She told him Emerald Isle would be half his and they would finish it together, but he said he didn't want any of her wealth as it belonged to her. "When Papa was dying he asked me to find Thomas. I didn't know who Thomas was or if I would ever find him, and all the time it was you, Desmond, he wanted me to find you. He mentioned you in his dying breath, you are Papa's son, my brother, therefore we share his wealth. How are we going to explain this to little John? I can never be his mother, but I will always love him. Life has changed for us, Desmond, but it will never change our feelings, they can't be taken from us," Emmeline said sincerely.

"We are back," called a little voice. Bridget Stenhouse wondered how Desmond was coping but she would talk to him tonight when little John had gone to bed. Emmeline stood up and said her farewells with their usual hugs; nothing had changed.

Everything was back to normal at Emmeline's stately home; Jane was amazed how she was coping with this truth. She buried herself in work at the coal-pit. One day while at her office there was a knock on her door. In walked a colliery safety inspector, who was visiting all the collieries in the area. It was Emmeline's collieries that were under scrutiny today. He had been down in the shafts and seen that all safety requirements were up to date, and that proper safety procedures were in place. "I see an award hanging in the entrance, what was that for?" he asked. Emmeline explained to him about Mr Ewan Fletcher and all the hard work he had put in to get a bill passed in Parliament to make the collieries a safe place for the miners to work. "We are so proud of him. Sadly he didn't live to receive the award, but all of us here remember him and what he stood for." "Your collieries pass with honours, Miss Christian, and the men speak well of you. Keep up the good work," he reported as he left. This visit was a result of Ewan's bill that had been passed. Now all collieries were to be inspected once a year, with no prior notice of when the inspectors were arriving. This was to catch out those who did not abide by the regulations and provide a safe workplace. Emmeline wondered how her uncles would fare with the reopening of their colliery. She had not heard from them since they signed her contract, but they must be paying the royalties, otherwise Mr Stenhouse would have contacted her.

18

Emerald Isle — the Warming Party

One year had passed and Emerald Isle was up and running. The mansion was finished, as were the gardens and the tree planting. It was used by herself, Desmond and little John at the weekends. They would catch the ferry across and spend happy times together. This was going to be Desmond's last semester teaching as he was going to come and work in an office at the coal-pit, now that he was a part owner. They had worked out with Mr Stenhouse how their wealth would be shared. Desmond wanted Emmeline to have Emerald Isle, as it was her dream. They would share the stately home and he and his son would come and live there when he finished at the school. Emmeline was happy about this as she would see a lot more of little John.

Mr Stenhouse had approached Miss Emmeline about inviting their friends over to the island for an island-warming party. This would put her right up there where she belonged, not that this worried Emmeline, although she thought the party was a great idea. He suggested they hire a chef for the night along with Jane and have a non-stop buffet that ran all night. Once it got dark the ferry stopped running so they would have to party all night. This was going to be a high society night, one that everyone would remember and talk about for many years. Miss Emmeline and Mr Stenhouse had been out several times over the past year with their friends, with nothing untoward happening. They were both on their best behaviour in each other's company and Edward made sure Emmeline's wine intake was minimal. He felt he was in control of her. The party was next Saturday night, and the guests would arrive late afternoon and party all night. There were beds for those that needed sleep.

Emmeline had gone to Ambleside for a day's shopping. She stopped off at her society friend that owned the haberdashery store. She could not believe the pretty pieces of clothing she had in her store. Some articles she had never seen before, therefore had to ask where on the body they were worn. Her knowledge of fancy clothing was very limited as she had no one to discuss these things with. Sadly, the only person that had seen beneath her outside clothing was Ewan. She remembered when she bought her new bodice and he had removed it from her body, and the warm feeling that had enveloped her. She wanted to look beautiful for her island party, so she sought the help of the friend. Emmeline thought some of her suggestions were a little over the top, but as she tried them on she could see how attractive she had become, especially to the opposite sex. She had never worn silk before and loved the feel of it against her body, especially the underwear. She spent up large as this was going to be her special night. She was now nearly twenty-one and had still not seen a naked body of the opposite sex. Was this about to change on Saturday night?

Everyone in Bowness knew that Miss Christian owned an island called Emerald Isle and it was the sister island to Isabella Curwen's Belle Isle. The townsfolk knew they were both heiresses, in fact related, with similar backgrounds. They were proud that this was their story to tell the tourists. Any story that boasted an heiress had to be told. Although they were a generation apart and Isabella Curwen had passed on, Miss Christian was still young, with her life ahead of her. There was a scandal in her family when an unknown illegitimate son of Mr Christian turned up and was entitled to some of his wealth. This made the story more exciting for the locals of Bowness.

Jane and the chef were already on the island preparing food for tonight's party. It was the talk of the town as there was no limit to the amount spent on food and drink. It was going to be a lavish affair. Mr Stenhouse was the brains behind all of this, as he wanted Miss Emmeline to be right up there with the best of society. He had been working on her for the past year. She had immersed herself in the running of her collieries, the miners were happy therefore her profit was accumulating; there was plenty for both her and Desmond. Mr Stenhouse was the one to benefit most from the truths that had been revealed, as he now had Miss Emmeline to himself and quietly in the background he felt he had her under his control. She and Desmond were still very close and this annoyed him a little. As brother and sister they were inseparable and little John now called Miss Emmeline 'Aunty Em'. Desmond had refused the invitation as they were not his type of people. He would feel uncomfortable.

The guests were arriving as they were limited to the timetable of the ferry leaving Bowness. Mr Stenhouse was on the first ferry to arrive and Emmeline was standing on the landing to welcome everyone to her island, Emerald Isle. Just the first glimpse he caught of her in all her finery set his heart racing. Why did she do this to him? No other lady had ever had this effect on him ... why her? She was so beautiful, one day he would take her to be his wife. As the guests stepped onto her island they all commented how beautiful she looked, and were aghast at the wealth that came with her. Although they knew her through their social gatherings, they never imagined such splendour. They were invited to wander around the island and through the mansion, as this was all theirs tonight.

The last ferry arrived and Emmeline greeted everyone, then she noticed George, who was once again unaccompanied. As she greeted him he pulled her close to him so he could feel the outline of her body next to his, then he whispered in her ear, "You look gorgeous tonight, my dear." She liked George, he was fun, but would her innocence lead her astray? The crowd mingled as they all knew each other, they were the elite. Emmeline was the unknown factor but after tonight that would all change. Because this was a social occasion, the formalities were dropped by Mr Stenhouse and Miss Emmeline. He was never far from her side as his heart was ruling his head and in his head, she belonged to him. George brought a glass of wine over for Emmeline much to Edward's disgust as he wanted to be in control. With this she wandered off with George and they walked among the trees. It brought back memories of her and Desmond dancing among the trees on Belle Isle, and she told George this. He thought it sounded fun to do something on the spur of the moment that came from the heart. They laughed as they shared their experiences. She could say anything to George, he was so easy to be around. "Emmeline, what is your relationship with Edward?" he asked. "We are just good friends, he told me one day he had found love, but I have never met his lady." "You are so innocent, Emmeline, you are the love he has found, he told me so," said George. "No, that can't be right, George," she said as she thought back to the night she made advances towards him and he rejected her. If what George was saying was right, why did he not like her touching him? "Anyway, he has never indicated his feelings for me, so I am free," she let him know. "That's good, Emmeline, because I am very interested," said a happy George.

Edward's eyes never left Emmeline and he was jealous watching the two of them obviously enjoying each other's company. Was she flirting with George? He made his way over and two became three. Emmeline excused herself to go to check on the food and to recharge her glass. This was her big night so she decided to let her hair down. She could fall into bed if things started to get out of control. Jane and the chef were organising the food and it wasn't going to be long before it would be out on the tables. Emmeline was talking to her friend from the haberdashery store about her selection of clothing she had bought when Edward appeared at her side. "Your lady has chosen some beautiful underwear, I hope you enjoy her choices,

Edward, you are a lucky man," she said. Poor Edward, he didn't know where to look. Why was Emmeline buying flash underwear? No one was going to see it. Emmeline looked at him and he looked away; no comments were passed. She was hoping to see a smile on his face, but this didn't happen. "For God's sake, lighten up, Edward, let your guard down," she said as she walked away. He was so stuffy at times, why wasn't he fun like George? He noticed she had filled her glass again; he would have to watch her.

Emmeline sought out George again, at least she could have a laugh with him; she wanted to feel happy. They walked to the end of the island together and sat down under a tree. George really liked Emmeline; she was gentle but she had a naughty sparkle in her eye. He noticed her silk bodice and wondered what else might be silk underneath her outer layer. He took her hand and squeezed it tight and while doing so he leaned over and stole a kiss. Emmeline enjoyed his attention; it had been a long while since any affection had been bestowed on her. She looked about her but nobody was in their vicinity. She leaned over and unbuttoned his shirt and put her hand on his chest and felt his heartbeat. This was all the encouragement George needed and his hand found her breasts. They felt soft and warm so he bent down and kissed them. That was when Emmeline saw Edward coming towards them so she quickly let George know and they sat up innocently. He sat down beside them and noticed that her glass was empty so he reached over to take it from her. She held on to it. Then his eyes spied George's shirt half unbuttoned; had Emmeline done this? Surely not! Why would she do this, why would anyone want to touch another person's bare flesh? This only happened in the bedroom of a married couple. "What happened to your shirt, George?" he asked. "I was hot so I was letting some fresh air in. If Emmeline had not been here I would have stripped to the waist," he answered. With this she burst out laughing. "I wouldn't have minded to see you bare to the waist, George," she said teasingly. Edward was horrified with Emmeline's comment. He would make sure she had no more wine.

As the night air set in and darkness was descending on the island, they all sat round and watched the changing moods of the lake. It went from being bright and happy to a sombre look as darkness crept across the water. A slight mist accompanied the darkness, which gave the lake an eerie appearance. Later when the moon appeared and shone down upon the water it gave it life and the waves danced with joy. By this time everyone had consumed a large amount of alcohol so there was a jubilant atmosphere across Emerald Isle. When midnight struck a silhouette of a naked man came towards them and as it came closer, there was George stripped bare dancing in the moonlight. Everyone cheered and clapped. Emmeline started to giggle, as this was the first naked man she had seen. Was this what Ewan was trying to hide from her, did he not want her to see this strange body part? She was intrigued and just stood and stared at George. He came up to her and took her in his arms and they danced around the trees. "See, Emmeline, spur-of-the-moment dreams can come true." And they both laughed. This was applauded by all.

Edward had been inside and when he came out to see what was so funny, he was horrified to see what was unfolding in front of him; he went into shock. There was his friend George dancing naked with his Emmeline and she seemed to be enjoying herself. He thought this was disgusting, while everyone else was laughing and encouraging it. While he didn't want to make a fool of himself in front of his friends, someone had to take control, so he marched over with a towel and told George to cover himself. "What's wrong with you, Edward, this is a party, we are celebrating the warming of Emmeline's island. Let her have some fun. This is probably the first time she has seen a naked man, am I right, my dear?" he asked. Everyone was waiting for a reply but she just stood and giggled. Edward took her by the arm and led her away. "What were you thinking, Emmeline?" "I like George, he is fun, and yes ,he was right, I have never seen a naked man before," she said angrily. "Neither should you. That is what marriage is for, it is sacred," he answered. "You are so old-fashioned and stuffy, Edward. Even when I made advances towards you, you ignored them, that hurt me. What is wrong with you?" With this Edward walked away. She knew she had hurt him but she had to say what she felt at that moment.

She went and mixed with the others as they were all having fun, singing and laughing. Next thing she felt arms around her and it was George. "I'm sorry if I embarrassed you, I had no right to ask you if you had seen a naked man, it is none of my business," he said. "But you were right, George, you are the first naked man I have seen. I got the giggles as I didn't know what to expect ... now I know," she replied and burst into laughter. "Was I that funny?" he asked. "You are fun, George, why isn't Edward like you?" "Something went wrong with his marriage. It lasted less than a month and she took off with another man. He has never spoken about it with anyone, so we don't really know what happened. It affected his self-esteem; perhaps he was a bit prudish and she may have made fun of him. He did say he found it hard to have any discussion on closeness and lovemaking. He thinks it should only happen when one is married and it is confined to the bedroom, but I tried to tell him different. The sad thing is, Emmeline, he loves you, but because you are younger and more outgoing he cannot bring himself to tell you of his feelings, probably for the fear of rejection." "But George, his stuffiness annoys me, it pushes me away. I tried to touch his bare skin but he got annoyed and told me it would never be discussed again." "Never mind, Emmeline, let us enjoy ourselves tonight. Edward has no claim on you. You can touch my bare skin anywhere, I will never complain." He quietly slipped his hand down the front of her dress and fondled her. Emmeline loved this feeling, she had missed this as it was now nearly three years since she had lost Ewan. She and Desmond had never physically touched each other apart from a hug and a dance among the trees on Belle Isle. At this moment she wished she and George were somewhere on their own, then she would ask him to make love to her; she now thought she knew what to expect and that she was ready.

Meanwhile Edward was down the other end of the island wallowing in self-pity. He so wanted Emmeline. In his mind she was his, but tonight he had been told for the second time that he was old-fashioned, and asked what was wrong with him. He had never seen or received any love from his parents. He didn't even have a say in his future — his father had told him what profession to take. Therefore, he was unable to express how he felt about anything. He so wanted to be like his friend George and now it looked like he had lost Emmeline to him.

Emmeline felt she had been mean to Edward so she wanted to find him and apologise. He was nowhere to be found so she decided to take a long walk and clear her head. It was then she spotted him sitting with his head in his hands. She crept up on him and put her arms around him. "I'm sorry for what I said earlier, Edward, I should learn to keep my thoughts to myself, I'm so young and silly at times. You are the sensible one." Just to hear her say he was sensible restored a little bit of his lost self-esteem. Now was the time for him to make his move and tell Emmeline how he felt, otherwise George was going to steal her from him. "Emmeline, I have fallen in love with you, I have felt this way for a long time but you were so young, you had to grow up so I waited. I want to make you my wife." She had never expected this, what a shock, as she thought he loved someone else. "But you told me you had found love, so I thought you had found someone," she said. "I found love in you, Emmeline, but I couldn't bring myself to tell you. You were still growing up. Did you know our fathers had planned for us to be together one day?" "What do you mean, Edward?" she asked. "When I took the firm over from my father, your papa asked me to stay on as his solicitor in the hope I might ask you to marry me," he said. This hit Emmeline right down in the very core of her heart. Did her papa really want her to marry Edward? She never knew this. Was it her papa's wish they would end up together? She loved her papa dearly; would this make him happy if she married Edward? "Why didn't you tell me this before, Edward?" "It has to be your decision alone, Emmeline." Her head was in a spin. Was this what her papa wanted, would it make him happy? She forgot her own feelings for the moment; perhaps she should accept Edward's proposal. Then she thought of George; he was fun. Could Edward ever be like him? Would he make her laugh and do stupid things with her? "I'm not good at expressing my feelings, Emmeline, but I will try," promised Edward. With this he took her in his arms and held her close. His thoughts weren't at all like George's; he didn't wonder what she was wearing beneath her outer clothes, he was just happy to be holding her. Would she be happy in an ordinary stable relationship or would she crave a little excitement? "Please think about my proposal, Emmeline," said Edward. With that he walked away and left her to think about what he had said.

Emmeline sat down and stared into the darkness. She could just make out the lights of Bowness in the far distance. What did the future hold for her? She now had her Emerald Isle just as Isabella had her Belle Isle, the only difference, she didn't have a husband. Two loves had been taken from her; all she had left was Edward and of course George. Would she be able to change Edward? Would he make her happy? Was this what her papa wanted? If she thought the answers to all these questions were yes, then she would say yes to Edward. But she didn't know!

As she was sitting there contemplating, she felt a hand slip down inside her dress. She was startled until she saw George. She removed his hand and told him that Edward had proposed to her. "I don't like to tell you this, Emmeline but you are his whole life, he loves you dearly. He is my friend and he has been hurt before. If I didn't care for him I would tell you otherwise, as I think I may have had a chance with you. This doesn't mean I will give up, because I won't, but he found you first." "Thank you for that, George, you have taught me so many things tonight," she said. "Tell me, Emmeline, was I really that funny that I made you giggle?" said George referring to his nude romp. "I don't know what I expected, George, but it certainly wasn't what I saw. I know now what to expect. I'm still in the dark about that aspect on life, but I guess I will learn."

"If you need any advice or lessons, I am always here for you. I'm only sorry it wasn't me who found you first," he said sadly. "If it was anyone other than Edward I would fight to the end for you, but I can't make an enemy of him, we have been friends for years." She stood up and gave George a thank you kiss, but he would not let her go without one last hug so he could feel her body pressing against his. He was sad it had to end like this, but he would be waiting in the wings!

Emmeline made her way back to find Edward, She was going to tell him she would accept his marriage proposal. It seemed the right thing to do; if her papa wished for it to happen, then he would be happy and so would she. She rang a bell for everyone to gather around, as she was going to give a speech. "Welcome, everyone, to my island. This has been my dream from when I was a little girl. Isabella Curwen was my heroine; I so wanted my life to be like hers. Our worlds were similar but there is one thing missing from my life and that is a husband, so the answer is yes, Edward." Everyone cheered and clapped and this added to the jubilation of the night. Edward made his way forward to be by Emmeline's side and gently kissed her cheek. "We want to see more than that, Edward!" someone yelled. It was Emmeline who came to the rescue; she took him in her arms and kissed him passionately. Then she addressed the crowd: "I cannot forget the people who have made me what I am today and that is the miners who work my collieries. I support them and the widows and children who have been left without breadwinners. As you all know I started a farmlet for them, it has grown in size and now they are able to feed themselves and sell produce from the land. The children who have had the chance to go to school, by you helping them with your donations, have done really well and now we are starting to see the benefits from this project. We are still accepting further donations to give more children the chance of an education. Thank you all, enjoy what is left of the night." This brought another round of applause. Edward was proud of his Emmeline but did he tell her?

Jane came up and gave her a cuddle and wished her all the happiness, God knows she deserved it. Emmeline found Edward and took his hand and led him up to her bedroom. As they entered she shut the door. "Come here and sit by me," she asked of him. She looked into his eyes and saw the fear that was building within him. "Don't be afraid, I just want you to tell me again how you feel about me." He looked at her and a tear escaped from his eye; this was the hardest request he had ever faced, how was he going to tell her? She sensed his frustration. "I will tell you how *I* feel. You are a good man, Edward, you are sensible and I was really happy when you told me you loved me, but I want you to tell me this many times as it is important. Please tell me again," she whispered. "This is so hard for me, Emmeline, I never saw love at home. I failed in my first marriage because of this, it frightens me to let my feelings known. But you make it sound so easy. I love you, Emmeline, I have been waiting for you to grow up and in that time, I nearly lost you twice. Now that I have you, I am still frightened." She took his hand and lay it on her breast. This was the first time outside of marriage he had touched another's flesh. "Tell me what you feel," she said. "It feels soft and warm, Emmeline." "That's what I want you to be able to tell me, I need to know how you feel." Edward could not believe what he had just done; it wasn't all that hard to tell her how he felt. Was his confidence slowly coming back? In fact, it felt natural to touch her. Emmeline left it at that; she didn't want to frighten him off so suggested they go downstairs and mingle with their guests. George came up to them. "You look after her, Edward, I'm waiting in line," he said as he winked at Emmeline. He felt happy for Edward but sad for himself, as he felt they had something going between them.

They all gathered at the lake's edge to watch the early-morning sunrise. By this time, relative quietness had descended on the island as tiredness had set in, and everyone was quite happy to relax and enjoy the moment. It was a peaceful ending to a wonderful night on Emerald Isle. Jane and the chef were busy preparing breakfast so all would be fed before they left on the ferry. The donation box for the children to attend school was full; this proved to Emmeline that these upper-class elite did care for the underdogs but they just had to be reminded. Emmeline had left an everlasting impression on these socialites, not that it mattered to her, but Edward liked to think he was one of them. As they all left the island they all thanked Emmeline for a wonderful time and hoped they could come again. George was the last one to get on the ferry; he was sad to leave and he hugged her in his usual style and he pushed his body into hers. She could feel something strange, but she thought she knew what it was ... a reminder!

It was back to the coal-pit office for Emmeline as one of the charge hands had to finish immediately as his wife was very sick; he had four children to look after. She had taken on his duties until Desmond could start working there. She had told Desmond and little John that she was going to marry Edward, and this hit a raw nerve with Desmond. He still felt deeply for her, it was more than a sisterly love.

He would give up all the inherited wealth to go back to how thing used to be, but with the raw truth, this could never happen. Little John asked her where she would live once she was married; would she still live with them in the big house? This was something that had not been discussed so she told him she didn't know yet. He hoped she was going to stay living with them. He and his daddy would soon be moving into the big home. This was going to be fun, as he could feed the horses and they could use the cart and carriages as they would be theirs. Little John didn't understand why, but Aunty Em had been very kind to them.

Edward had asked Emmeline to accompany him to Ambleside today so they could buy their ring. He brought his carriage to the front entrance and helped her up onto the front seat so she could ride beside him. They drove to town together both in a happy mood. Edward told her he didn't want a long engagement, and would she be happy to set a wedding date in the not too distance future; this she agreed to. When they got to town they made their way to the goldsmith's store. Emmeline looked at the rings and one stood out above the rest; she tried it on and knew that was the one. She asked Edward what he thought and he bent down and kissed her cheek in agreeance. She couldn't believe what had just happened; was he showing his feelings? So she reassured him: "Thank you, Edward, that was nice." He asked the salesperson to put the ring in its bag as he wanted to place it on Emmeline's finger in private. They went around to the haberdashery store so Emmeline could discuss with her friend about a wedding dress. On the way home Edward pulled to the side of the road and stopped the horses. He took the ring out of his pocket and took her hand and put it on her finger.

Emmeline leaned over and kissed him and thanked him for being so thoughtful.

19

Emmeline's Wedding

There was only one week to go until Emmeline's wedding day. Her dress was almost finished, so she was driving to Ambleside often for fittings. It was handy to have Desmond at the coal-pit, as he took over when she was busy with her wedding arrangements. He was compassionate towards the miners, and would go down the shafts to see that the safety procedures were in place. This was as important to him as it was to Emmeline. They worked well together: he would never fall out with her as he respected her; she was his boss as he was still learning. When little John came home from school, Jane was there to care for him. He loved living in his new home and spent a lot of time at the stables with the groundsman as he loved the horses. He would do his homework at the big desk in Aunty Em's office, as he felt important sitting in the rather large chair. From his upstairs bedroom he could see the lake. It was so much fun living here.

Edward and Emmeline agreed that they should live in her stately home, as they felt they couldn't take Jane away from little John and Desmond. If there were any problems they would move to Edward's, although he liked the thought of living in this prominent home as it was known by the townspeople as Mr Christian's stately home. Edward would bring his horses and carriage up to Emmeline's stable as they were of the best and her groundsman would care for them. It seemed the logical solution as she loved living there. Her bedroom was large with a dayroom off it, so they would have their own privacy. Jane had now moved in fulltime so she gave up her lodgings.

Emmeline's friend from the haberdashery store was going to be her matron of honour and George was Edward's best man. Little John was the page boy and he was so excited. There were very few family members to invite as the only living relative Edward had was his Aunty Bridget, Desmond's mother. On Emmeline's side were her uncles and their families, but they were not going to be invited. She had kept in touch with a couple of her boarding school friends, and they were excited to get an invite, as they were dying to meet Emmeline's man. Today she was meeting George in town for lunch as they made the final wedding preparations. She was excited about this as he always made her laugh. This was the final fitting for her wedding dress; it looked beautiful and she was so happy. She bought pretty underwear to wear on her wedding day so when she undressed it would be on show for Edward. She hoped he would like what he saw, as he was still having trouble expressing his feelings.

Once she was finished shopping she went to the local inn to meet George. He was waiting for her. "Hello, my dear, I have missed you," he said as he gave her his trademark hug. He always made her feel happy down in her heart, he was so bright, but she had to stop comparing Edward to him. They were two totally different people. He wanted to know how Edward was, had he lightened up any now that they were close to getting married? He felt Emmeline would be wasted if Edward remained stuffy. "Oh, a couple of times he has let his guard down but I will have to work on him. Letting his feelings be known does not come easily to him. I am wondering how he will be on our wedding night, I don't know what to expect. If I hadn't seen you naked I would have got a shock, so thank you, George! Ewan and I loved touching each other; we would lie together with our bare skin touching, but he would not let me touch below his waist, as he didn't know if I had seen a man's parts. I told him I hadn't. I loved him so much I wish we had made love, then I would know what to expect." "But Emmeline, each man is different. If you had made love to Ewan, you might be disappointed with Edward, so it's best you didn't. If you find that love is not what you think, then come to me," he told her. They finished lunch and it was time for her to drive home. George helped her up onto the front of the carriage and let his hand brush her bottom area; he didn't apologise because to him it was a naughty but natural act of affection.

The ceremony was going to be held down by the lake. Emmeline decided to close the collieries for the day and let the miners and their families be part of their celebrations. They would still be paid. For all her wealth she never forgot those that helped her make it. She would have loved to have been married on Emerald Isle, but to ferry everyone across the lake was not a possibility; it would mean the miners' families would miss out. She wanted all those that were part of her life to share in this wonderful day with her and Edward. She had given the catering to the local inn, who had hired extra staff as there were going to be a lot of mouths to feed. There would only be one table and that was for the wedding party; all the other guests were provided with forms to sit on as Emmeline wanted the upper class to be seated with the working class. There was to be no discrimination, all would be as one on her wedding day. This is what she wanted although Edward thought different. People that knew Emmeline would understand as she never forgot her workers; they were just as important as the upper class.

Jane was preparing food to go over to Emerald Isle for Miss Emmeline and Mr Edward as this was where they were going to honeymoon. She had offered to come to the island with them, but Emmeline wanted her to stay and look after Desmond and little John. She wanted to be on her island alone with Edward. She was hoping for some excitement. Would he dance with her around the island and lie in the grass with her? Was she setting her hopes too high?

Today was Emmeline's big day. The sun was shining and the lake was calm; this was especially for her, as nature wanted to share its good tidings with this special person, one who didn't discriminate between the rich and the poor. All the townspeople were excited. This was one of their own, their heiress, who would be remembered for many years as was Isabella Curwen. This area had produced several heiresses and this made them very proud.

Emmeline's friend who was her matron of honour had arrived with her wedding gown and Jane was helping Emmeline to dress. Desmond was attending to little John with his suit as he was so excited. Her friend had made a headdress of fresh flowers which she pinned into Emmeline's hair. She looked radiant; surely this would make Edward's heart race. When Desmond and little John saw her come down the stairs they were stunned; she looked beautiful. Desmond's heart gave a little flutter, and the old hurt came back. Little John told Aunty Em she looked like a princess.

It was time for the wedding party to climb into the carriage and be driven to the wedding venue by Desmond. The carriage looked classy as it had been decorated with ribbons and fresh flowers, even the horses were wearing ribbons. The whole town turned out to see what their heiress Miss Christian was wearing. The minister, George and Edward were waiting down by the lake for the carriage to arrive. As they pulled up and the wedding party stepped down from the carriage, cheers rang out. Emmeline looked the 'picture perfect bride' in her beautiful white lace gown as she and her party walked towards the waiting groom. Edward was amazed by the image that stood before him; she was beautiful and within minutes he could claim her as his wife. She stood and looked lovingly into his eyes, hoping to see the look returned ... but did she? The minister started the ceremony by welcoming everyone to this important gathering today and before long the couple were repeating their wedding vows to each other. Little John handed Uncle Edward the ring and he placed it on Emmeline's finger. The minister announced them as husband and wife. "You may now kiss the bride."

They made their way up to the local inn where all the

seating was set out. The bridal party sat at the wedding table. As they were being seated, Emmeline noticed a group of children led by Desmond lining up in front of their table. She recognised them as the children that she had sponsored for free schooling. One of the older girls spoke on behalf of the group: "We all wish you the best for the future, Miss Christian. Thank you for making it possible for us to attend school as it has given us a choice, one which without your kindness we would never have had. We love you, thank you for believing in us." She reached out to hold Emmeline's hand. Emmeline stood up and walked around and hugged the speaker. "Thank you all for coming today. All children deserve the right to attend school and I will continue to support this cause. Here today we have people who have given generously to help the children; would you all stand up, please, so we can see you." With this the upper class stood and the working class applauded them. This was a meeting of all classes today; each person was just as important as the person next to them. This was how Emmeline saw life. Edward was so proud of his wife. Everyone loved her, she was full of kindness for people from all walks of life — something he did not see within himself.

George stood and gave a speech which brought laughter all round ... but that was George! He gave Emmeline a special message. "Emmeline, you are the dream I have let go, but Edward deserves you, may you both be happy and love each other." As he sat down she noticed a tear slip down his cheek. Then the matron of honour stood and said her speech: "I have never met such a caring person as Emmeline. She has never forgotten her roots, she cares for her miners and took to heart the plight of the underprivileged children. She is a pillar in this community. I wish you and Edward all the best for a happy future." This brought cheers and claps from all those attending.

After they had eaten, Emmeline left the bridal table and went to catch up with her boarding school friends. They hugged each other and had so much to catch up on. When Emmeline told them that Edward was her father's solicitor, the man she had met while on one of her visits home from boarding school, they all laughed. They remembered how she had described him, which wasn't very flattering. But when she told them what had happened to her two lost loves, they felt sad for her. "Did you get your dream island, Emmeline?" they asked. Yes, she told them, that part of her dream had come true but other things hadn't worked out. She asked them to come back one day and stay on Emerald Isle with her. They made a promise to do so.

It was now time for the bridal couple to catch the last ferry over to their island. Everyone came down to the lake front to see them off and wish them all the best. Emmeline looked radiant as she boarded the ferry and Edward stood with his arms around her. Little John yelled for her to come back soon and this brought laughter. George and Desmond, on the other hand, both felt sad, as this was a final goodbye to a lost love ... lost to someone else!

As they stepped off the ferry Edward took the bags and they walked up to the mansion. He asked Emmeline to wait until he had unlocked the doors and put the bags inside. He then came out and lifted her and carried her across the threshold. She was so happy. Jane had set up food for them to have supper. Emmeline noticed that Edward was a bit uptight so she poured him a whisky, and a wine for herself. They sat out on the porch and talked about the day. "I am very proud of you, Emmeline, you are so loved by many people; I never realised this until today. It was good of my friends to mix with the common people, they don't do this very often, but this was special for you today." "As I have said, Edward, to me there are no classes of people, everyone is equal; it is just that some people have more opportunities than others, thus allowing them better lives. We will always differ on this, but I will never change." They sat in silence. Edward had never heard Emmeline talking like this before.

Darkness was setting in and a cool breeze was descending on the island. They went inside and Emmeline suggested they go upstairs as she was feeling tired. Edward went and poured himself another whisky. He told her to go upstairs and he would be there shortly. She had visions of them walking the stairs together hand in hand, then rushing to the bedroom where she would undress and let Edward see her naked body. Where had those dreams gone? Edward watched his beautiful Emmeline climb the stairs, then he had a panic attack. He remembered his first marriage on his wedding night; he couldn't relax therefore his body parts weren't able to function. His wife ridiculed him and he lost his self-esteem. Sadly, during their month of marriage, he was never able to perform, so she left him. He had never spoken about this to anyone, not even George.

What was going to happen tonight with Emmeline? He swallowed down his whisky and wondered if he should have another to settle his nerves ... yes, one more! As he made his way upstairs he expected Emmeline to be in bed. When he entered the bedroom, she was standing by the window and he could see the silhouette of her body through her underwear. She turned around to face him then slipped out of her underwear so he could see her naked body. He stood still as if frozen on the spot and gazed over her body; she was beautiful. He couldn't move, tears were forming in his eyes, and with this he felt panic. Then a strange feeling came over him; he felt his body changing so he knew then that all was okay. He undressed and when she saw his naked body her mind went back to George; this is not what she saw, this was different. Edward took her to the bed and they lay together with their bodies touching. Edward knew Emmeline didn't know what was about to happen so he was gentle with her. She just relaxed and let him do what he had to do. He was pleased that his body allowed him to complete his manly duties, so there was going to be no problems with Emmeline. Because she didn't know what to expect, what had happened was not anything like what she had imagined. Edward seemed to enjoy himself so she was happy for him. She was left feeling disappointed, but for Edward's sake she would say nothing. Perhaps it would be better next time. What happened to the magic feelings she felt when Ewan touched her? Then she realised Edward hadn't touched her body; he had just taken what he wanted.

When Emmeline woke the next morning, Edward was not in bed. She got up and bathed and went downstairs. He was in the parlour making breakfast. "Thank you for last night, Emmeline, that was wonderful. We will make love often." Emmeline went up to him and kissed him. She didn't know what to say about last night, so it was just as easy to seal it with a kiss. This was an unspoken answer; therefore her feelings would not be discussed. They walked the island hand in hand and stopped every so often and held each other in their arms. Her thoughts went back to last night. She loved her body being touched and caressed, but this had not happened; she wasn't sure how she felt about what did happen.

They had lunch, then went upstairs to lie on the bed together and relax. Edward told her to undress as he was doing, then he took her in his arms. She lay there waiting on him to touch her body but instead he pulled her over to him then climbed on top of her and again did what he had to. Emmeline lay there hurting and willed back her tears. This was not what it was like with Ewan — he kissed and caressed her, they loved each other, he excited her. Would his lovemaking have been any different? she wondered. Was this all there was to it? Did she imagine too much? Now she would never know. Edward was her husband.

That night they sat together on the grass and watched the sun go down. It was putting on a lovely display of colours for them and Emmeline felt warm and romantic, so she took off her top and bodice and put Edward's hand on her breast encouraging him to caress her. Next thing he had taken his trousers off and pulled up her dress and was lying on top of her. It was then she realised this was her life from now on, of hurt and selfishness. Edward was a man who pleased himself.

The next morning, he caught the ferry over to Bowness for the day to check-in at his office. Emmeline stayed on the island and cried most of the day. What was happening between her and Edward was not what she expected her life to be like. What happened to love as she knew it with Ewan? They were two totally different men: Ewan was caring and working class, Edward was upper class and cold. She couldn't change anything now, she was his wife. Could she speak to him about what she wanted from him? She would try next time they were intimate.

Emmeline organised what they were going to have for supper when Edward came home. She went down to wait for the ferry. She saw it coming and Edward was standing waving to her. She was happy to see him so they walked up to the mansion hand in hand. As soon as they got inside Edward asked her to come to the bedroom with him. He took down his trousers and asked her to get undress and get into bed. She did as she was told, then he climbed on her and had his way. She didn't have the courage to say anything to him. They then got dressed and went down to have supper. He told her he had work to do at the office so he would have to go back in a couple of days. He poured himself a whisky and sat down on the settee. Emmeline poured herself a wine and sat next to him. She put her arms around him and closed her eyes; there she was with Ewan, she could see his beautiful eyes with that naughty sparkle that made her heart melt. Tears welled up in her eyes. She reached up to pull his head down so she could kiss him. "What are you doing, Emmeline?" With this she opened her eyes and there was Edward. Her beautiful memories were gone and her warm feelings were replaced by a coldness. Edward was tired and asked Emmeline to come to bed with him. She could think of nothing worse at this moment so said she would be up shortly. She poured herself another wine and went outside to breathe in some fresh night air. With this the memories of Ewan came flooding back and she sat and relived them over and over again. She hoped Edward would be asleep by the time she eventually went to bed.

The next morning Emmeline woke first so quietly got dressed before Edward woke. She decided to go for a walk on her own around the island. She was missing Jane, little John and Desmond. If Edward was going back in two days' time she would go home too. Her honeymoon had not turned out as exciting as she had imagined it might have been. As she looked back over time she should have seen the warning signs with Edward; he was not a warm, lovable man, but she did hope she could change him. He wasn't a bad man, just perhaps too sensible and very selfish. He didn't think of others' feelings, but she had seen this, as he had no time for the working class. He considered himself above them. Perhaps she had married the wrong man ... where was George?

The night before they were to leave the island Emmeline asked Edward if they could dance around the trees and be a bit silly, do something out of the ordinary. He looked at her with hostile eyes. "You only want to remember the night you danced with George naked. I will not lower myself to his level," he barked, and made his way upstairs. Emmeline didn't mean any malice by this suggestion so she followed him upstairs. "Sometimes I don't know what you are thinking, Emmeline," he told her. She was furious with him; now was the time to tell him a few truths. "Edward, I want you to caress me and kiss me, play with me before you climb on top of me." "I'm sorry, I have been selfish. Come to me?" he said as he held out his arms. He undressed her and kissed her body and touched her secret parts, which stirred up those missing feelings, then he made love to her. She squealed in delight; this is what she imagined love to be.

The next morning they boarded the ferry to return home. For the first time since arriving on the island she felt happy. Last night was wonderful. She actually felt a tiny bit of love for Edward. She hoped it would continue. Everybody was pleased to see Emmeline home again. She had missed little John and all his questions but no one was happier than Desmond. He missed her terribly. The collieries were fine; it was in the home he missed her most. Although she was married to Edward he could still share time with her. He hoped the three of them could still go over to Emerald Isle for the odd weekend without Edward.

Since Ewan's safety bill had been passed there had been no more colliery disasters. The safety inspectors could not be bribed, as they were not self-employed like they used to be. Before the bill was passed the bosses could divert the course of justice by paying the self-appointed inspectors to bypass their collieries. Now each colliery was registered, so all inspectors had to record the safety of each colliery. If this was not obeyed their jobs were on the line. At last the miners were protected and their work places were safe. Edward tried hard to persuade Emmeline not to go to the coal-pit now that Desmond was working there. He thought she should be more of a lady. His position was well established now as he owned Emmeline and her share of her papa's wealth.

Six months of marriage had passed and Emmeline was feeling poorly. She had always been a fit and healthy person, but some mornings she found it hard to get out of bed. At night when Edward tried to climb on top of her, she felt sick and pushed him away. He did not take kindly to this as this was his right. Jane noticed Miss Emmeline was not herself so she asked her if she was with child. She was shocked to hear Jane say this, as she and Edward had not talked about children; she didn't know if he wanted any. She decided to go to the doctor and he confirmed that she was at least four months with child. She was in denial; how was she going to tell Edward?

That night as they went to bed she asked him if he wanted children. "I am not ready yet, Emmeline, this is my time to bed you." She had to tell him. "Edward, I am four months with child, you cannot bed me until we have had our baby." "What do you mean, Emmeline? You never discussed this with me!" he yelled. "I'm sorry, Edward, I didn't know," she sobbed. With this he ripped her clothes off and bedded her. Desmond heard Edward yelling followed by Emmeline sobbing. He felt sick inside; what was happening to Emmeline?

The next morning, he waited for her to come downstairs. She looked ill. "What is wrong, Emmeline?" he asked her. She burst out crying so he went over and put his arms around her. "I am with child," she sobbed. "That's wonderful news," he said in earnest. "Edward is not happy, he is angry with me, but I didn't know." At this moment Jane walked in and saw Miss Emmeline in Desmond's arms. He reassured Jane that he was just comforting Emmeline. She broke loose and ran up the stairs to her bedroom. He told Jane what had unfolded and she was angry with Mr Edward.

20

A New Era

Four years later Emmeline and Edward had two children, a son Charles and a daughter Sarah. They now had a nanny as well as Jane. Edward insisted that Desmond and little John move out of their home. Emmeline arranged for a new home to be built on the adjourning land so they could share the gardens and the stables. Edward was not happy with this arrangement, as he felt Desmond knew too much of what was going on in their private life. Emmeline defied Edward's wishes and she and Desmond went ahead with the build. There were still some decisions that were out of Edward's control and he didn't like this. He now considered himself as head of Emmeline's wealth. As much as he forbade her to go to the coal-pit, as he thought this was beneath her standing in society, she went. Ever since the night he raped her when she told him she was with child, she had never forgiven him. He still demanded his right to bed her when he wanted it. This was his marital right so she obeyed him, but hated him a little more each time it happened. Their marriage had now turned into a marriage of convenience. Emmeline was unhappy; all that she dreamed of had not materialised. She found herself walking up the hill more often to visit Ewan and wishing they could still have been together. He was her one love. She loved her children; they gave her a reason to carry on. Little John was now twelve years old and he loved the little ones. Often she and the children and Desmond and his son would spend a weekend on Emerald Isle without Edward. This was when they had the most fun.

Edward spent more of his time mixing with his upper-class friends. George had moved away so they didn't see him any more. Emmeline missed him terribly. She still had her school programme for the underprivileged children and her farmlet for the widowed women. The farmlet had grown five-fold and now was providing a decent income for the families as well as keeping them in food. She didn't often attend Edward's social gatherings any more as she preferred to spend the time with her children. She still had her friend at the haberdashery store but because she belonged to the upper class, Emmeline never told her what was happening in her personal life. She would sell her beautiful underwear to wear for Edward, which Emmeline brought home and hid away in a drawer. He didn't need any encouragement, he took her when he needed her, in a manner that was not to Emmeline's liking; he was physically hurting her.

As she thought back over her life with Edward there were signs right at the start that should have sent out warnings to her: his coldness, his controlling ways and his disregard for the working class. Even now it was beneath him to talk to miners; he would never go near the collieries. Emmeline was so annoyed with him as these were the people that were keeping him in a lifestyle that he so enjoyed.

When Emmeline found she was with child again with her third child she was pleased as this meant Edward would leave her alone. She wouldn't have to put up with his continuing roughness. One afternoon he came home from work earlier than usual and found Emmeline sitting on the floor playing with the children. She looked so happy, this was his beautiful Emmeline. He asked her to come upstairs to the bedroom and he shut the door. He undressed and told her to get into bed. Emmeline told him she was with child again. He became enraged and grabbed her and threw her on the bed and raped her. This was the end for Emmeline; she told him never to come back to her bed, ever.

He stormed out of the home and went to the stables and hitched the carriage to the horses and rode off. He was so mad with Emmeline, but more so with himself. Why had he become like this? He loved her, she was a good dutiful wife and doting mother. He had noticed lately she was spending more time up the hill visiting Ewan's grave. He was having flashbacks to his childhood days when he saw his father treating his mother the same way. Many times he had walked in on his father hurting his mother, why was he doing the same? He vowed he would never treat a woman like this. He drove from Bowness to Ambleside and went to the inn where he hitched his horses to the rail and went in to have a few whiskies. Hours later he was still downing the whiskies. Then it was time for the inn to close so he had to leave. He unhitched the horses and climbed up on to the seat with much difficulty. He started on his way home but was not fit to handle the horses. He was angry so he reached for the whip and cracked it above their heads. This frightened the horses and they reared up throwing Edward to the ground.

The next morning when Emmeline woke she was alone in her bed. Edward must have got the message. She dressed and went down to see the children. There was a knock at the door and Jane attended to it. It was the groundsman wanting to know if Mr Edward was at home as the horses were loose and still had the carriage attached to them. "Miss Emmeline, is Mr Edward at home?" enquired Jane. Emmeline went upstairs to the guest room but the bed hadn't been slept in. She came downstairs and said he wasn't there. She went and spoke to the groundsman and let him know Edward wasn't at home. He decided to take the carriage and go and look for Mr Edward. Emmeline was still hurting after last night; she didn't care if he never came home, as she was frightened of him. His demands on her were out of control, but she had told no one. Jane had guessed things were not good between them; she worried for Miss Emmeline.

Later that morning the groundsman arrived back with Mr Edward in the carriage; he had found him lying on the roadside outside of Bowness. He was unconscious. Emmeline went with him to the doctor; she was so embarrassed as he stunk of whisky. The doctor said he had to go to hospital straight away as he was very ill. They took him to the hospital and were told to come back tonight, by then they might know what was wrong with him. They drove home. She had no feelings left for Edward, he had brought everything on himself. She had been a faithful and dutiful wife to him and still he abused and hurt her.

A week later Edward was still in hospital. He had

suffered a stroke and was partially paralysed down his left side, limiting his speech and movement. He was being sent home from the hospital the next day for Emmeline to look after. She was dreading the thought of him coming home. While he was lying in hospital she saw him for what he was: the coldness in his eyes and the relentless demands he made on her, he was a stranger. She had arranged for a home help to come in and look after him. She was eight months with child so couldn't help lift Edward. She still wanted to spend a little time at the coal-pit as it was her outlet.

The next morning Desmond came to the hospital with her to help lift Edward. They helped him to the carriage, but he didn't want Desmond there and demanded that Emmeline help him. Desmond told him to behave himself as she was in no state to lift him, he would have to get used to other people helping. Edward didn't like this so started to perform. They closed the carriage door and Emmeline climbed up on the front seat with Desmond and rode home.

While they were riding home, Emmeline told Desmond what had been happening between her and Edward, that he had continually raped her. He was horrified, and said it would never happen again, as long as he lived next door. If he was out of place, to come straight over and he would deal to him. "He is only half a man now so you shouldn't have too much trouble with him. Don't let him bully you, hit him with something if he gets out of hand," said a concerned Desmond. He never liked Edward as he always thought he was a class above everyone. When they pulled up outside the front entrance Jane and the nanny had the children there to greet their papa. Desmond and Emmeline helped Edward out of the carriage, but he was abusive to Emmeline as she had not ridden with him. She took the children inside as she was shocked at Edward's behaviour. How was this going to affect this household? Desmond helped him inside and sat him in a chair; he was protesting all the way expecting Emmeline to help him. The children came up to their papa and put their arms around him. "You're home, Papa," they said. He let them sit on his knee, but his eyes were cold, especially when he saw Emmeline. He had hatred in his eyes, this was all her fault. If she hadn't got with child this would never have happened.

The household was in chaos. Edward demanded to sleep with Emmeline in their bed, but he wasn't able to use the stairs, so they had set up a guest room downstairs for him. She would never ever share a bed with him again. She hated him. This was the last straw; he screamed blue murder. Emmeline felt safe in her bedroom, with him unable to climb the stairs. This was her saving grace. He was able to do little things for himself but dressing took him forever as his movements were very slow. He needed help to bath. The first day home Emmeline help him to bath, but he kept trying to grope her. She felt sick that he wasn't about to give up on his demands on her. That was the end. The next day she started the home help, who was an older lady who had dealt with such men before. She would deal to him, there were ways and means. He hated Emmeline for this. He could shuffle along with the help of a walking stick, but his speech was quite slurred. He couldn't do much except sit or lie down. It was only a week away before Emmeline was due to give birth. She spent a lot of time playing with the children. Edward would sit and watch them laughing. His behaviour had quietened down and he enjoyed seeing the children happy. They had a calming effect on him and would climb onto his knee and put their arms around him. This was the only love he received now.

Emmeline went into labour during the night so Jane called Desmond to take her to the nursing home. By the time they got the horses and carriage ready she was in strong labour. They only just made it in time as the baby was born within the hour. It was a little boy. Emmeline looked at him and said, "Hello, baby George." She had decided she would give him the surname of Christian, not Stenhouse, and if something happened to Edward she would get a royal pardon and change the other children's names from Stenhouse to Christian. God knows she needed a little bit of joy in her life, and baby George would bring that ... if only in memories!

When Emmeline was discharged from the nursing home Desmond was there to pick her up. He drove her and the baby home in the carriage. The nanny had the other children waiting to see their new baby, but Edward was nowhere to be seen. They all hugged baby George, they loved him. When Emmeline walked inside, Edward was sitting in a chair. Physically he wanted nothing to do with this baby. In his mind he caused this all to happen; if Emmeline wasn't with child, then that night would never have happened. Now the blame had moved from Emmeline to this new innocent little soul. He pointed to the baby and said, "Edward." "No, this is baby George," she told him. He started yelling, "Edward! Edward!" With this Desmond came in and shook him. "Stop that, Edward," he said. With that he got up and shuffled off to his room. This was when the home was the happiest, when Edward was not present. Jane was happy to see Miss Emmeline back home. She knew there would be no more babies, as now she knew what had been happening between Mr Edward and Miss Emmeline. She hated Mr Edward, he was a horrible man, to think he abused Miss Emmeline all that time and she had told no one. She was a brave soul.

Baby George being the newest member of the family received all the attention. Even Charles and Sarah forgot their father in favour of the baby. Edward's anger was building; he was receiving very little attention and virtually no love at all. He hated the name George and disliked the child. Then when he saw Emmeline holding the baby, kissing and loving him, he would sit and cry. She hardly knew he was present as he was dead in her mind. She had very little to do with him, as her memories of him were best forgotten ... all of them! She was afraid to leave the baby unattended because of the ice-cold look in his eyes. She had seen those eyes before. Emmeline made this known in the household. At no time was baby George to be left on his own in Edward's company. His crib was upstairs in Emmeline's bedroom where he was safe.

Edward became so full of hate, he continually upset the household. Every time he saw the baby he would yell, "Edward! Edward!" If it was the last name left on earth, Emmeline would not have used it on this innocent little soul. The next few days came and went and Edward continued to turn the household into chaos. Until one day it all ended! Emmeline went upstairs at the end of the day to go to bed. She checked on baby George and he was sleeping, so she climbed into bed and fell asleep. She woke to Jane calling, "Come, Miss Emmeline, it's Mr Edward." She quickly dressed and opened her bedroom door and stood at the top of the stairs, and there was Edward lying still at the bottom. She noticed his walking stick at the top of the stairs and felt sick. Had he made it to the top then fallen? What if he had made it to her bedroom, who would he have hurt first, her or baby George? She froze until Jane called to her. "It's all right, Miss Emmeline, he's dead." Emmeline burst into tears, not for Edward, but in sheer relief that this 'evil' would be removed from her home and from her life.

She asked Jane to make the necessary arrangements to have him removed. The nanny kept the children upstairs in the nursery until Edward was taken away. Emmeline would not feel completely safe until she saw him buried under the ground. She didn't want him buried on the hill. She would feel his cold eyes gazing down upon her every time she went to the window. Emmeline arranged the burial to take place in Ambleside; the further away the better. The whole household was happy that Edward was no more. He was a blight to this family.

That afternoon as Emmeline sat and watched her children playing so happily in the nursery, her thoughts went back to each time she told Edward she was with child. He had raped her in absolute rage. She couldn't understand why! Thank goodness she had no ill feelings towards the children, as they were the innocent ones. She didn't have the joy of a loving supportive husband to share the fruits of their love ... all she had was hurt!

On the day of the funeral the lake was choppy as if in anger. It was flinging its spray high into the air, as if it wanted rid of it. This was the exact mood that came over Emmeline. Jane had put the children into the carriage and Emmeline joined them. Desmond and little John rode up the front with the groundsman. An eerie silence had befallen on them all, no one wanting to mention his name. As they pulled up at the burial grounds a crowd of

Edward's upper-class friends had gathered. Emmeline hadn't given her miners the day off to attend, as that would have been hypocritical; he had no time for them, so she didn't expect them to have time for him. She saw the funeral carriage arriving with the coffin and she felt a cold shiver creeping down her spine. He was still haunting her, but not for much longer! In a few minutes he would be gone for good. Edward's friends carried his coffin to its final resting place. The minister spoke kind words about him, so she let him have his final glory. As they lowered the coffin down, Emmeline took the children to the graveside for them to say goodbye to their papa. Baby George was too young to know what this gathering was all about, which was just as well, as his father blamed him for all that had happened. She had to see the earth put over his coffin; only then could she feel safe.

Unbeknown to Emmeline there was someone in the crowd who watched with interest to see if any tears were shed by her. He watched her intensely and saw a cold look in her eyes as the earth was being put over the coffin. This wasn't like the Emmeline he used to know. What had happened? She still looked beautiful and he felt a happiness in his heart. He never forgot how she giggled when he did his naked appearance that night on her island. He had taken her in his arms and danced around the gardens with her ... yes, it was George! So, she and Edward had two children, what a lucky man to have had such joy. He had never settled with anyone as the only person he wanted, he gave to his best friend. She was a warm loving person and liked to do crazy things, just like him. That was why he shifted away; he couldn't trust himself and didn't want to hurt Edward.

He watched as Emmeline cuddled her children and then

he noticed she had a baby in her arms. How sad for Edward to have left behind such a young child. The after-burial function was held at the Ambleside Inn, as Emmeline didn't want any reminder of 'him' at her home. The day he was carried out, that was the end! The groundsman drove them around to the inn. Emmeline just wanted to go home but out of respect, a word she could not associate with Edward, she decided to attend for a short while. His upper-class friends made a fuss of the children, which was what they needed. Then they all talked about how much he would be missed. Tears streamed down her face upon hearing these words, tears of hatred, tears of pain. "Can I wipe away your tears, my dear?" said a voice from behind her. She knew that voice!

He took his handkerchief from his pocket and wiped the tears from her eyes. "You look sad, Emmeline, I'm so sorry to hear about Edward. Who is this dear little soul?" he asked. "This is baby George," she told him. "You didn't forget me then, Emmeline?" he asked. "No, George, never," she said as her tears flowed. She just wanted to go home. "George, please give me a little time, then come and see me. I have so much to tell you," she sobbed. She gathered up the children and said her goodbyes, and left. Everybody understood why she left as they thought her tears were for her loving husband Edward ... nothing could be further from the truth.

The day following the burial Emmeline decided to take the children and their nanny to Emerald Isle. She asked Jane to go through the home and removed every reminder of Edward; she didn't care what she did with it, but she wanted everything gone by the time she returned. This was one request that Jane was only too pleased to do, as she hated Mr Edward for what he had done to Miss

Emmeline. Before she left Emmeline asked the groundsman to remove Mr Edward's horses and carriage, to take them to the farmlet and give them to the widows and their children. They would now belong to them. They could use them to take their produce to the markets in Ambleside on a Saturday. They would be very thankful for this small act of kindness … given out of hatred!

The next few days on the island gave Emmeline time to bond with her children and to show them she loved them completely. A little extra love was given to baby George as he was the one most hated by Edward, and this tugged at her heart. Her fear was slowly disappearing; he could never hurt her again. At times she escaped the children and walked to the other end of the island and would sit in the very spot where she and George sat. The daydreaming was starting to come back to her. She remembered unbuttoning George's shirt and slipping her hand down his chest and feeling his heartbeat. Then she felt George's cold hand touching her breast and she sat up as a warm shiver ran down her spine. She had not had these feelings for almost seven years. But this was not right, she had just buried her husband. She quickly brushed those memories aside, she must mourn … but for what?

The children loved coming to the island. At night they would all sit and watch the sun as it slowly got closer and closer to the water, then it would disappear. "Where does it go, Mama?" they would ask. Emmeline told them it went for a swim each night. As young as they were, she told the children about Belle Isle and their relation Isabella Curwen who was an heiress and who built the rounded mansion they could see.

It was time to leave her island and go back home. She felt her sense of belonging was slowly returning. She hoped all trace of Edward would be gone. Jane was happy to have the family come back home. It was lovely to see Miss Emmeline looking happy. She had removed all the physical evidence of Mr Edward, it was as if he had never lived there. All that was left for Emmeline to do was get rid of his business and sell his home. One of his friends was looking after the business while he was sick, but now he had put an offer in buy it. She accepted the offer with no bargaining, it had to go at whatever price. Edward's money was 'dirt' money to Emmeline and she wanted nothing to do with it, it was all going to help the underprivileged children. Not that he would have been pleased about that, as that was helping the working class who he didn't think helped themselves. This would see that all the children had the chance of an education.

Emmeline had started back at the coal-pit for the mornings, as Desmond had persuaded her to once again take an interest in her collieries. The miners were always asking for her to come back, they all missed her, she just brought a little bit of finesse around the men. Charles had started school and Sarah missed him terribly, so now she turned her attention to baby George. Emmeline spent the afternoons with her children, after all that had happened, they were very dear to her. This weekend they were going over to 'Emerald Isle'. They would catch the last ferry over on Friday.

Today was the day. As they were packing to get ready, Jane came into the drawing room and told Emmeline there was a strange man in the garden who seemed to be planting a rose bush. Did she know who it might be? Emmeline looked puzzled as she hadn't bought any plants for her garden. She looked out the window, and her heart missed a beat. There was George; what was he doing? She ran to the entrance, down the steps and into the garden. "George, what are you doing?" she yelled in excitement. He dropped the shovel and the next thing they were in each other's arms. Jane watched from the window as this all unfolded. Who was this man? Miss Emmeline seemed to be happy to see him. They seemed to be in each other's arms for a long time, then she saw the man gently kiss her cheek. Obviously, they were more than just friends. Yes! She had seen him before, it all came back to her; the island, that was where it was, he was a friend of Edward's. "I have brought a special rose for you, Emmeline, and I wanted to plant it in your garden, so every time you look out your window you will think of me. When you said at Edward's burial that you had never forgotten me, I wanted to give you this rose. It is called Remembrance. "Oh, George, you are such a dear, so thoughtful." "I have come down for a few days. I wanted to see you, I couldn't stay away any longer. Is it all right for me to be here, are you still in mourning?" he asked. "George, the children and their nanny and I are going to the island for the weekend; we leave in an hour as we have to catch the last ferry. Come with us, come and stay the weekend, I have so much to tell you." George didn't know if this was in fact a good idea. He thought back to the last time they were there and he remembered what happened. "Can I trust myself, Emmeline?" he asked of her. They both laughed. He said he would go and pack a bag as he was staying at the inn. He would meet her at the ferry.

Emmeline was so happy, she felt feelings stirring in her body. It was now seven months since Edward had passed away, but these feelings had been gone long before then, long, long before then. They hugged each other again and then Jane saw the man leave. Emmeline came in and asked

Jane to put extra food in the basket as she was having a guest for the weekend. He was coming to the island with her and the children. Jane could see happiness in Miss Emmeline's eyes, something she hadn't seen in a long while. The groundsman had the cart waiting to take them to the ferry. Jane hugged her and told her to have a lovely time. They picked Charles up from school on their way, then they were dropped at the ferry. George was already there waiting. He helped load the baskets onto the ferry then helped them to board. Emmeline told the children that George was going to be staying with them for the weekend and they would have a lot of fun. She knew George! Charles went and stood by George and next thing they were holding hands. This brought tears to Emmeline's eyes as she didn't know if Charles was missing his papa or if he felt safe with George. When Sarah saw Charles and George holding hands, she went up to him and reached up for his other hand. Here was a total stranger befriending her children. Their own father never held their hands ever while crossing on the ferry. As soon as Sarah saw Belle Isle, she told George that it all belonged to Isabella Curwen, and they were related. She was a very wealthy heiress. This made him smile as she was oblivious to the fact that her mother was also an heiress.

As they landed at the jetty, George helped everyone up then lifted the baskets off. He wouldn't let Emmeline carry the heavy baskets, he said he would come back for them. They walked to the mansion and Emmeline unlocked the door. By this time George and Charles were on their way back for another load. Charles was like George's shadow. While Emmeline set up the food in the pantry, George and the kids went out to play ball together and laughter was ringing out over the island. When had she last heard such happiness? Not since the island-warming party had laughter sounded so warm and comforting; it brought life back to Emerald Isle. Emmeline, the nanny and baby George stood and watched the fun and they smiled at each other. She went and made a room up for George and put his bag in it, then she attended to supper for them. "Come, everyone, time to eat," she called. They all sat around the table and ate. George couldn't understand that Edward's name had not been mentioned once, even by the children; this was most unusual. "Did your papa play ball with you when he was here?" he asked the children. No one answered, they just looked at each other. Emmeline asked the nanny to bath the children and prepare them for bed. She went and picked up baby George and gave him a big kiss and cuddled him. George took him from Emmeline and bounced him on his knee, much to his glee. Emmeline was overcome with tears; Edward disliked this little soul so much, and here was George playing with him. He looked up and saw the tears. "Is it all right for me to do this, is something wrong?" he asked. "Oh George, if only you knew," and she burst out crying. The nanny came and took baby George. "Don't worry, Miss Emmeline, I will tend to the children, you stay and talk," she said.

Emmeline's sobbing grew louder as she thought about what she was going to tell him. "Sit down, George, you have to know about Edward. When he died I was freed from hurt and rape. I was happy he died," she cried uncontrollably. "What do you mean, Emmeline, did he hurt you?" "It began from the day he married me. He started to control me, he took from me and gave me nothing, I was just there to be used when he wanted me. With each child, when I told him I was with child he raped me in anger. He hated baby George, in fact the night he died he made it to the top of the stairs. It makes me sick to think what he might have done to the baby or me if he hadn't fallen back down the stairs. I was so relieved when I saw him lying there, and when Jane told me he was dead, I was happy. I hated him that much. I was scared of him, he got worse and no one knew. I didn't tell anyone for a long time, but in the end I told Desmond. That is why I buried him away from me and the children. I didn't want to go to his burial but I had to make sure he was under the ground. Only then could I feel safe again," she cried. "Oh Emmeline, I am so shocked. The bastard, but why, why was he like that, did he go mad in the head? Edward, I can't believe that of him. I knew he was stuffy, we all did, but not cruel. I fully understand why you are relieved he is dead, no man deserves to live when he behaves like an animal, the bastard!" With this he took her in his arms and they cried together. "My poor Emmeline, why didn't I stay and fight for you, I gave you to him trusting he would love and care for you, instead he abused you. All those years I dreamed of you and Edward and I was jealous that you were so happy. I have suffered too, Emmeline, but not as much as you. How can I ever forgive myself?" he asked. "Let us say goodnight to the children then we can come out onto the porch and talk some more." "I'm so happy you are here, George," she said. They tucked the children in and Emmeline gave them their goodnight kiss. That wasn't good enough, they demanded a kiss from George. The nanny was attending to baby George. Emmeline kissed him and told him she loved him dearly. She told him this every night, knowing how much his papa hated him. She felt she had to love him twice as much.

Emmeline told George all about her life with Edward, how she asked him to touch her before he bedded her, which he did it once and never again; how he would demand her at any time and when she wasn't willing he would raped her. Once he knew he could assert his marital rights, he became the master and he enjoyed hurting her. He wanted to keep her the dutiful wife, just as his mother had been. He would never look at her naked body, it was of no interest to him. Even when he had his stroke he wanted to take from her. Emmeline was just thankful that he couldn't climb the stairs, that was until that fateful day. That day his life ended, her life began again.

George was in shock, he had never heard of such behaviour before, but of course no one talked about it, so how would he know? They sat talking into the wee hours of the morning until George suggested it was time for bed. He kissed Emmeline goodnight and went to his room. As she undressed that night she looked at herself in the mirror. Her body shape had changed since she had the children, and this was the first time she had noticed. Her firm body was no more, and it was a bit plump around the middle area. She still desired to be touched and caressed, and it was only since she had seen George again that she even had such thoughts. They were dead until now; her heart had turned to stone many years ago. As she tucked up in bed she felt warm and safe.

She woke the next morning to yells of laughter. She climbed out of bed and went to the window and there was George and the children playing ball again. Emmeline was shocked when she saw what time it was; half the morning had gone. When she came downstairs they had all had breakfast; she was the last one to eat. Baby George was crawling around on the grass, and the nanny was with him making sure he didn't eat any bugs. Emmeline ate a quick bit of breakfast then went outside to watch the children playing ... all three of them! She had never seen them so happy. This is how she imagined her life would be. She sat in the sun and felt its warm rays penetrating her skin through to her heart. It was warming, the big thaw had begun.

After lunch they all went for a walk around the island. George carried baby George on his shoulders to give the nanny a break. He had taken a liking to George and pulled his hair so he would make a noise, then he would smile. When they reached the spot that held past memories for Emmeline and George they stopped and rested. George took her hand and squeezed it letting her know he remembered what had transpired here, then he let her go. He didn't want her to feel any pressure from him, as she had to recover from her past horrors. They continued on their walk and when Emmeline took baby George, the other two children claimed a hand each from George; he had become their firm friend. This is what Emmeline had expected Edward to do with his children, but that never materialised. He never expressed his feelings towards the children. It was only after he had his stroke that he encouraged them to sit on his knee and cuddle him, as this was the only love he received. He never learnt that to receive love, one must give love.

Just before supper Emmeline poured herself and George a glass of wine. The children were lying around as they were tired after their walk. "Where did you go, George, when you left Ambleside?" Emmeline asked. "I went to Barrow-on-Furness and bought into a nursery, and did very well there, but I always wanted to come back to Ambleside or Bowness. I love the Lakes District." Emmeline was happy to hear George was going to settle near them. They had supper and played games with the children until it was their bedtime. George asked her if she would like to take a walk with him and they would watch the sunset. Emmeline let the nanny know. They walked along the lake front and found a sheltered spot where they sat together to watch the sun go down. George put his arm around Emmeline and she cuddled into him. The sun's rays shone on the water creating a pattern of colours that took on a shimmering effect; it was quite spectacular, and oh so peaceful! Then all of a sudden it disappeared into the water for its evening swim. With this the evening breeze sneaked in from the south, bringing with it a fine mist. They decided to head home and go indoors. Everyone was in bed.

Emmeline asked George to come and sit with her on the settee, where they cuddled up together. She felt safe in his arms. All fears from the past were forgotten, this was the effect George had on her. She wished she could unbutton his shirt and slip her hand down his bare skin and feel his heartbeat, but she was afraid. Perhaps it wasn't proper at this time; was it too soon ... too soon for what? It was seven months since she had been widowed. Since when had she felt so relaxed and happy? She looked at George's shirt buttons, they looked tempting! A tingling feeling ran through her body, she wanted him, she was ready, she needed to be loved totally. "Come to my room, George," she asked of him. She got up and took his hand and they went up the stairs together. She closed the bedroom door and undid her bodice, then lay on the bed. He lay beside her and caressed her neck then her shoulders, and down to her breasts. She loved this feeling, this is what she wanted from Edward, to be touched. George was so gentle, he made her feel wanted and loved. He didn't want to rush Emmeline as he didn't know how much hurt she was still carrying. She asked him to move his hands further down her body to her secret parts and touch her there. She slipped off her underwear. George slowly worked his hands down her body. She had never felt these sensations before, this was all new to her. He played with her and she wriggled around in the bed. "I'm ready now, George, please bed me," she begged. "Are you sure, Emmeline? I won't hurt you." He stood up and took his clothes off. Emmeline knew what to expect. She closed her eyes and waited for the pain. Instead, George was so gentle with her, what she felt was pleasure, pure joy! Tears rolled down her cheeks. "That was beautiful, I was waiting for the hurt, you didn't hurt me, George, thank you," she said. He could not believe what he had just heard. Oh my God, how she must have suffered; he hated Edward. He held her close, he loved this girl, she deserved better. Then he wondered if this was why Edward's first wife left him; did he treat her the same, did she suffer? No one would ever have known his dark past, or what he saw as a child, as he never talked about it, he never told anyone. He had harboured dark secrets all his life unable to let them out, or seek help. In his own mind he loved Emmeline and when he found he could perform his marital duties with her, he became obsessed. At last he felt masterful and took control, getting his pleasure from hurting her. He was jealous because everyone loved her. What a bastard, thought George.

George and Emmeline must have drifted off to sleep, as they woke to two children standing by the bed asking George to come and play. "Shoo, go away, we will be there soon," said their mother. They left and closed the door. Emmeline couldn't believe what she felt last night, and she asked George to make love to her again, now. He obeyed and they romped around in the bed until that wonderful feeling came back. Emmeline's demons were gone forever, she was a complete woman again. George had taught her so much last night. She totally loved him.

It was time for them to leave the island. The fairy-tale dream had come to an end. They boarded the ferry and headed back to Bowness. Emmeline stood with her arms around George and the children cuddled into them both. She couldn't believe she could feel so happy, she was so in love with him. As they tied up at the wharf George helped lift the baskets out of the ferry and put them on the wharf. Emmeline's groundsman had arrived with the cart, so they loaded it up and all climbed aboard and rode back to Emmeline's. Jane was there to meet them and she was pleased to see the man was still with them. "Jane, this is George, he is our friend, we had a neat time with him, he played with us all the time," said Charles and Sarah. She had never seen them so happy. "Come, George, and see our rooms." And they took his hand and led him away. "Oh Jane, we had the best time ever, the kids love George, he was so good with them, they were so happy," she told Jane. "And what about yourself, Miss Emmeline, did you have a good time?" Jane asked. "Yes, the best time ever," she said with a cheeky smile on her face. Nothing else had to be said. Jane got the message loud and clear. Was the household going to turn into a place of happiness at last?

21

The Finale

Emmeline had talked George into staying for a further two days. She didn't want him to leave. She wanted to love him many times over. She loved the feeling it left in her body; she felt worthy and wanted. She even started to love herself again. Jane asked where Mr George was going to sleep so she could make a room up for him. "Don't worry, Jane, George will sleep in my room with me." Nothing more was said; Jane's thoughts had been confirmed. Emmeline found George out in the garden pottering among the roses. This was his job, he loved working in the garden. Then the children pestered him to play the ball game with them. Laughter rang out as they hit the ball and chased it. Never had there been such joy in the grounds of this stately home.

As they were getting ready for bed Emmeline suddenly remembered all the beautiful underwear her friend talked her into buying to make Edward a happy man. Forget

Edward, it would now be for George's benefit. She opened the drawer and took out the silk underwear and put it on while George was in the bathroom. When he walked out and saw Emmeline he wanted to touch her all over, then undress her, she looked so inviting; he loved nice underwear, as well Emmeline knew. She remembered when he asked her what else she was wearing that was silk. She had never forgotten as she loved his comments; they were personal. Another fulfilled night was had. Emmeline thought this was a wonderful pastime; she was making up for lost time, she had never known such love. She always remembered Ewan, he was her first love, but it was a different kind of love. This was complete love, what she felt for George.

George was saying goodbye as he had to leave; the children were sad as was Emmeline, but he would be back. They had talked things over and Emmeline had asked him to come and live with them fulltime, as her husband. She loved George, she had done so for many years, but she wouldn't admit it to herself as long as Edward was alive. Now she couldn't imagine life without him. Of course, he had to face the fact that Emmeline was an heiress, and a businesswoman. He loved the children and he loved her. Yes, he wanted to marry her and love her for the rest of her life.

Desmond had to get used to the idea of losing Emmeline again. Right from when Edward was sick he was her main support. She called on him when she needed him and he felt the closeness they once had. He tried, but he couldn't let go. It could never be, but to live next door and work with her, he felt part of her life. He had never found another love. Little John was now big John, so Emmeline's children had become a big part of his life; he loved them as his own. He enjoyed working at the coal-pit as he was a kind person and like Emmeline he cared about the miners. They would go out together to the farmlet and help out with the animals and make sure the widows and their children were getting by. Because there had been no more colliery disasters, the widow population had stayed pretty much the same over the past few years. However, there were still miners dying of coal dust consumption, but this was always going to be an ongoing problem. It was associated with working in the collieries.

Many of the children who had received the free education put in place by Emmeline had moved away to find a better life, as now they could at least read and write. There were the ones that only ever wanted to be miners, like their fathers and forefathers before them. It was a family tradition. The girls especially benefited, as other than to become housemaids and nannies there wasn't much future for them. Now they had a choice. That was what Emmeline wanted for them ... to have a choice!

Today Emmeline and George were getting married. It was a family gathering. They wanted a quiet affair, they didn't need all the pomp and ceremony, they just wanted each other. The children were excited as they were getting a new papa, and they loved George. They never mentioned Edward's name and neither did Emmeline. He was history!

The newlyweds were on their way to Emerald Isle for their honeymoon. The children were left at home with Jane and the nanny. This was their escape for a few days. They crossed on the ferry and made their way up to the mansion. After Emmeline had finished putting the food in the pantry and organising the home she called out to George, but he was missing. She went outside and called him. Then in the distance she could see a figure, and as it came closer she saw a naked man running towards her. He gathered her in his arms and they danced together between the trees. He whispered to her, "Remember, Emmeline, spur-of-the-moment dreams can come true." This was her wonderful fun-filled George. He picked her up and ran into the home with her in his arms. He tried to take the stairs but tripped and they both ended up in a heap at the bottom of the stairs. Emmeline ripped off her clothes and begged George to bed her right there. She was so excited she couldn't wait; this is what she had dreamed of secretly, to do crazy things, and she knew George was just the one to want the same. It didn't take him long to undress as he had come prepared; it was times like this when she didn't need to be touched and she was ready to be taken by this tender, loving man.

That night Emmeline sat on the porch and looked across to Belle Isle. She remembered telling her beloved papa the day he left her that she would own her own island one day. All her life she had dreamed that her life was going to be the same as Isabella Curwen's. But this was not to be! On her path she had experienced a lot of pain and suffering, but now she had found the happiness she dreamed of. She owned Emerald Isle, a sister island to Belle Isle. In the end, the Lakes District's two heiresses, Isabella Curwen and Emmeline Christian, were afforded lives that were similar ... but different!

About the
Author

Margaret Nyhon lives in Alexandra, in the Central Otago province of New Zealand, where she writes, paints and practises the crafts of printing and bookbinding. She has worked extensively in hospitality management in New Zealand and resort management in Australia. The urge to trace her family history led her to the writing of her first non-fiction work, *de Marisco*. She has written several fiction and non-fiction works. Margaret is married and has three adult children and two grandsons.

Other Books by
the Author

Non-fiction

de Marisco
Freedom Knows No Boundaries
A Wake-up Call
A Shattered Dream Across the Tasman

Fiction

Isobella (Book 1 in the *Isobella* series)
Isobella: Self Redemption (Book 2 in the *Isobella* series)
Coming soon — Betrayal by an Irish Rose

Acknowledgements

Thank-you for your time and patience Morgan, my cover girl!

To my publishing team Martin and Eva.